THE WALLFLOWER LIST

ABOUT AN EARL
BOOK ONE

JESS MICHAELS

For Michael, who always sees me, no matter how many walls I hide along.

PROLOGUE

Marianne stood beside the dancefloor, back pressed to the wall, watching as couple after couple spun by. Her isolation was not unusual, it was how things had always been since she had come out two years ago. Due to a great number of circumstances, including gossip, death and her own shy disposition, the exercise had been a failure. She'd felt it keenly at the time, but now...well, now it was almost comfortable. Especially when she was joined at the wall by her dearest friend and fellow wallflower, Lady Claudia, the sister of the Marquess of Broadsmoore.

"Did you see the feathers Miss Percy has in her hair?" Claudia asked as she handed over a glass of watered-down punch and smiled at Marianne.

Marianne shook her head. "I don't think so."

"Oh, if you did, you'd know," Claudia giggled. "They're huge. I heard she poked poor Sir Niall in the eye when they were dancing and he nearly fell over."

"Where is she?" Marianne asked, and lifted on her tiptoes, now desperate to see this fashion faux pas in with her own eyes. Not that she had much ground to stand on when it came to that score. Her own gowns were lovely, of course, but she'd never given much time to the current fashion of low necklines and lifted bosoms and all-in-all flashy and reckless exposure. She didn't feel confident enough.

"She's standing with Lady Charlotte, the Marquess of Chilton's daughter," Claudia said, pointing to a stunning red-haired woman across the room.

"Lady Charlotte always looks so pretty," Marianne sighed. "I wish I had half her fashion sense. And her absolute certainty in every step she takes. Oh..." She finally saw the aforementioned Miss Percy, or rather her feathers and *then* Miss Percy. They were at least two feet long, dyed pink and they flopped around her face and everyone else around her. "Gracious, she's going to injure herself and others!"

"You know, if she poked out the eye of Prudence Green, at least she couldn't see to find victims for her cruelty." Claudia grabbed her arm and they both began to giggle over the potential demise of a young lady who hadn't been very kind to them.

Marianne sipped her punch and continued to look around the room. She smiled as she caught a glimpse of her brother Finn, standing across the room with his best friend, the Earl of Ramsbury. Sebastian looked utterly dashing, as always. Though when he turned to a lady beside him and leaned in to whisper in her ear, her heart sank.

"Looking at the two wicked earls?" Claudia asked.

Marianne rolled her eyes. "I cannot call my brother a 'wicked' earl. He isn't wicked. And even if he were, I wouldn't want to know about it."

Claudia laughed again. "Anyway, all you ever look at is *Sebastian*."

"He's my friend, that's all."

"Of course he is." Claudia rolled her eyes.

A playful elbow to her friend's side was all the defense Marianne could make to the implied charge. "Honestly, I should never tell you

deep, dark secrets. You are absolutely atrocious to bring up such topics."

"I never brought anything up, you did by mooning after him," Claudia corrected her, and then sighed. "Honestly, he is very handsome."

"Of course he is. And it isn't as if I'm the first person to ever notice it. But I know my place, Claudia, and it's here along the wall. I'm his friend and that's all I shall ever be. I'm very clear on that."

Claudia was silent for a moment, her gaze troubled as she continued looking out into the crowd. "Don't you ever want more than the wall?"

"More?" Marianne repeated. "You mean like marriage and children and the like? I suppose that's a hope for the future. Something *might* change. You know a few of the wallflowers have matched with very nice widowers in the past few years."

"No, not that," Claudia said, and her tone was tense now. It was such an odd thing, for Marianne wasn't accustomed to her being anything but playful and kind.

"Then what?"

"What about *adventure*?" Claudia said while clasping her hands together before herself. "Romance? Something out of the ordinary that would shock the world?"

"You sound like you're talking about a scandal," Marianne said.

"Oh, how I'd love a good scandal," Claudia sighed, but then she smiled at Marianne. "You are pale as paper. Does the idea shock you so much?"

"I've experienced a scandal," Marianne said softly. "I can't recommend it."

Claudia put an arm around her and squeezed. "Of course you have, I wasn't thinking. It was silly of me. I suppose I've been reading too many gothic novels where young ladies like us land the wicked rake like Ramsbury or cause a delightful outrage at a garden party all to solve a murder or…or catch a ghost? Whatever the last one was."

"It was a housekeeper pretending to be a dead woman in order to torment a lady," Marianne said. "Which I think wouldn't be as entertaining in real life, although I suppose I could try. For you."

They laughed together and all the tension and longing was gone from Claudia's voice as she said, "Come on, let's go out on the terrace and dance in a dark corner. We might as well have some fun tonight."

Claudia caught her hand and together they hurried out onto the terrace for some girlish fun where no one would judge. Marianne loved her friend for always lifting her spirits, even if some of her ideas were a little mad. After all, wallflowers like her and Claudia didn't strike out on adventures. If they hoped for them, it was likely to end in disappointment.

So she just had to enjoy the life she was living. It was for the best.

4

CHAPTER 1

Five Years Later

There were five people at the funeral of Lady Claudia. Five. Marianne knew the exact number because as she stood on the edge of the grave, umbrella dripping fat, cold raindrops onto the shoulder of her stiff, itchy mourning gown, she continually counted them. As if somehow more people would materialize. As if somehow *someone* would show up late and rush to reveal that they had cared for Marianne's best friend as much as she had.

But the number remained constant. Five.

Six if one were to count Marianne's great-aunt Beulah. Which she did not since her aunt had only come to chaperone Marianne and had gone back to wait in the carriage the moment the skies had opened up with their own version of mourning for Claudia.

So five the funeral party remained.

Marianne blinked back tears. It was all so unfair. Claudia had taken ill just a few scant weeks ago. And now she was gone and of the *five* people in attendance at her final farewell, Marianne was the only one who did not look distracted, bored or anxious to depart. Even Claudia's elder brother, the Marquess of Broadsmoore, seemed preoccupied. The moment the preacher ceased his droning words about ashes to ashes and the Lord's will, the marquess turned away and began to thank the few people who had bothered to show up to the service.

Marianne stayed just where she was, staring down into the cold, dark hole where her friend's coffin had been lowered. Soon it would be covered in dirt and then…well, then there would be no pretending that Claudia was not dead. That somehow this was a terrible dream.

"Lady Marianne?"

Marianne blinked, startled by the sound of the marquess's voice and the gentle touch of his gloved hand on her elbow. She turned toward him with the faintest hint of a smile. It was all she could manage at present.

"I'm so—I'm so sorry for your loss," she managed to choke out.

Claudia's brother was an older man and as he nodded the lines on his face deepened with emotion. At least he offered his sister that. "Thank you, Lady Marianne. And I am sorry for yours. I know you and my sister were as close as two people could be without sharing blood."

Marianne sucked in a breath in order to keep her tears inside. She wasn't about to shed them here in front of people who could clearly not care less about the loss of her best friend. Well, some didn't care. All but the marquess had already begun to roam back to their carriages to escape the rain. They couldn't even grant Claudia the respect of getting wet.

"She was my dearest friend," Marianne managed to respond with great difficulty.

The marquess nodded slowly. "I know she would have said the same of you. Don't think I don't appreciate how wonderful and true a friend you were in these last years of her far-too-short life. Claudia obviously felt the same, for she has left you a small token of her affection."

Marianne blinked up at the older man. This was utterly unexpected. "A token?"

"Yes." The marquess smiled softly. "It is a jewelry box she kept on her dressing table. I believe our late aunt gave it to her upon her sixteenth birthday. Claudia left special instructions that it was to be bequeathed to you."

Marianne lifted her hand to cover her lips as her thoughts turned to Claudia's room. How often she had admired that exact box as they readied themselves for parties or giggled together like the silly girls they certainly no longer were. All those memories were so dear to her now.

"I know the piece you are referring to. It was a favorite of mine," she whispered.

"Then it is good it will go to you. I shall have it sent over to your home this very afternoon. Will that be agreeable to you?"

Marianne nodded. "Of course, thank you."

"Well, thank you again for being a true friend to my sister." The other man glanced up at the departing mourners, none of whom could seem to get to their carriages fast enough. "She had few close companions. May I escort you back to your vehicle?"

Marianne glanced back. Her aunt had probably fallen asleep by now, slumped over against the door as she was wont to do whenever she got into a carriage for more than five minutes. "No, thank you, my lord. I believe I shall stay here a few moments longer and say a last private goodbye."

The marquess looked at her for a long moment and in his eyes Marianne thought she saw a flash of guilt. And why not? She knew Claudia had never been any closer to him than to anyone else in her life. Let him feel the twinge of regret that he had not treated her with more kindness or love. "Very well. Goodbye, Lady Marianne."

"Goodbye, my lord," she said to his retreating back, and then turned back toward the open grave to whisper a few last words to her fallen friend.

~

S ebastian, Earl of Ramsbury, took a long swig of whisky from the glass his best friend had provided and grinned. "Excellent."

The Earl of Delacourt turned toward him with a half-smile. "Yes, it's a fine bottle, that is for certain. Worth every pound."

"A good thing, too, since I'm sure it set you back more than a few." Sebastian set the glass aside. "After supper, what do you say we go find a few more drinks and perhaps some feminine company? We could go to the Donville Masquerade or another hell."

Delacourt sighed. "I would dearly love to do so, but I don't think that will be possible tonight. It's Thursday—my sister will be joining us for supper."

"Ah, yes, one of my favorite people," Sebastian said with a careless shrug. It wasn't as if he was hurting for women. One tonight, one tomorrow, it was all the same to him. "Why does she always join you on Thursdays again?"

"Our great-aunt hosts a weekly gathering with her sewing group at Marianne's home." His friend grimaced. "And my sister may be a spinster herself, but not so far into her old maidenhood that she enjoys four hours of listening to those women cackle endlessly about how we should all still be wearing powdered wigs."

"No, I cannot imagine your sister finding much entertainment in such a thing. Her wit would be wasted on such mundane topics."

Sebastian couldn't help but smile. He had known Marianne for almost twenty years, since he and Delacourt had become friends at school. She had been just a girl then, but a bright and funny one. As all three of them grew older, Sebastian had come to appreciate her sharp observations and quick mind. She was the only woman he had ever met who he considered a friend and she truly *was* one of his favorite people.

Delacourt's butler stepped into the room. "Lady Marianne, my lord."

With that, he stepped aside and allowed Marianne to come into the room. Sebastian set his drink down as he stared at her. Although he couldn't say that his friend had ever been at the height of fashion, tonight her plain black bombazine gown was drab and lifeless in the lamplight. It made her pale face look positively ghostly, as did the flat way she had fashioned her brown hair, pressed tightly to her scalp in a bun at the nape of her neck.

"Great God, woman." Sebastian laughed. "What in the world are you wearing?

Marianne lifted her gaze to him and Sebastian was shocked to see tears clouding her dark eyes. He had never seen her so emotional.

"My dear friend Claudia was buried today," she said softly.

Sebastian dipped his chin in shame. Damn, he had heard that news a few days before and wondered vaguely why the passing of such a mouse of a wallflower should resonate with him. But of course, it was because of Marianne's close relationship to the woman.

Delacourt stepped forward and placed a hand on his sister's shoulder gently. "I'm so sorry, Mari. And even more sorry that my business today kept me from acting as your escort to the funeral, myself. How was the service?"

Marianne shook her head and removed the glass from her brother's hands. Sebastian watched in surprise as she took the last sip of his whiskey. She made a brief face that said liquor hardly ever touched her pale lips and then shrugged.

"Short, impersonal and poorly attended," she answered with a frown that made her brown eyes even more forlorn and empty. "Claudia deserved better."

Delacourt opened his mouth to say something, but before he could, the butler returned to the room.

"I'm sorry to interrupt, my lord, but the message you have been waiting for has arrived."

Delacourt sent a brief glance to his sister and then bowed

slightly. "I hope you two will forgive me. This message is related to some business and it is important."

"Of course," Sebastian said as he waved his friend away. "Your sister and I are quite capable of entertaining each other."

He sent her a playful look that normally Marianne would return with a laugh, but today she did not glance up from her focused stare at Delacourt's empty glass. As her brother left the room, she didn't even acknowledge his exit.

Sebastian sighed. There were many things he was quite talented at when it came to women. Seduction came to mind. Dancing, flirting and compliments came with such ease that he could hardly remember a time when he didn't have such things right on his tongue and ready to use.

But comforting...*that* was not his forte. And clearly it was what Marianne needed in that moment.

He stepped closer. "I feel I owe you an apology," he began.

Those words snapped Marianne from her fog and she glanced up at him with surprise. "*You*? Apologize?"

She laughed and the sound sent great relief through Sebastian. He preferred his friend to be light again, not muted and sad.

"Yes," he continued, and reached out to take her hand.

Marianne's gaze came up to his in disbelief and Sebastian's astonishment matched the expression on her face. Her hand was ungloved and he realized he had never touched her skin before in all the years they had known each other. They had danced, of course, she had taken his arm as escort from one room to another, but there had always been a layer of cloth and propriety separating them.

Now that his flesh touched the warm silkiness of hers, the intimacy of that gesture was deeper.

"Truly, Marianne, I was insensitive when I mentioned your mourning gown," he said softly, surprised by how easily the words came. Comfort might not be his strength, but in this situation it came far more naturally than he ever would have guessed. "I *had* heard of the loss of your friend and I should have recalled it when I saw you. My deepest condolences."

Marianne blinked at him and her surprise faded, replaced by the return of her sadness, but also the warmth of appreciation. "Thank you. Of all the people who said that to me today, I think you might be the only one who meant those words."

He tilted his head. "Do you remember what you said to me when my uncle died?"

Marianne's eyebrows drew up in surprise. His uncle had been the only person in his painful childhood who had not failed him. As such, he was not a topic who often came up. Sebastian made sure of it, because it was too difficult and vulnerable, so he understood her reaction.

"I said many things, as I recall," she whispered.

He smiled as memories of her kindness that day almost seven years before flooded him. "You did, all of them helpful. But the one that did the most good was when you told me that the pain would never be erased, but that it would fade and mellow with time. That it would become part of the fabric of my being, the last gift from an uncle to his nephew."

Marianne's chin tilted down. "Yes, I do recall that."

"And it was true," Sebastian said quietly. "As it will be true for you eventually. Take some comfort in that."

"Thank you." Her gaze flitted up. "I think perhaps her passing would not hurt as much if I hadn't realized…"

She trailed off and Sebastian found himself leaning forward in curiosity. "Realized?"

She shook her head slightly. "I realized today that Claudia… perhaps like—like me…meant very little to anyone else. But she meant the world to me. And I miss her greatly."

Sebastian's brow wrinkled. He didn't like that she compared herself to the emptiness of Lady Claudia's death. It was as if Marianne thought that no one would care if she were suddenly gone, which wasn't true at all. Was it? *He* would care, her brother would care, even that batty aunt of theirs who shared Marianne's home would care.

She blinked to send away the tears that had returned to her eyes. "I'm so glad you're here tonight, Sebastian," she said with a wobbly smile. "You are exactly what I need to feel better."

Sebastian cleared his throat. He doubted there was another woman in the world who would say such a thing to him and not mean her words with an intensely sexual twist.

"Oh? And how shall I make you feel better?" he asked.

Marianne smiled. "You will tell me some terribly ribald tale and turn my tears into ones born from laughter before my brother returns. You are the only one who will allow my maidenly ears to be burned by such talk and I think it would make me feel so much better tonight."

Sebastian tilted back his head and laughed. He did delight in telling Marianne naughty stories, if only to see her blush and swallow and stammer. Though he did tone down his jokes and tales quite considerably, whether she recognized that fact or not.

He leaned forward, closer to her ear. She smelled of lemons and the faint hint of roses, a charming combination that was fresh and light.

Quietly he began to whisper a joke he had recently heard told in a pub in a humble part of town. And while he toned down the language and took out at least one lightskirt from the punchline, in the end Marianne still blushed to the tips of her ears and covered her mouth as a giggle escaped past what had been pale and pinched lips until that moment.

"Sebastian, that is *terrible*," she finally said when she could manage words.

At that moment, Delacourt returned to the room. He frowned and Sebastian recognized why in an instant. His friend was always irritated when Sebastian stood too close to his sister. He wasn't the only friend who felt that way, of course. With his reputation, Sebastian supposed he deserved it, but great God! He and Marianne were friends. He had never considered her more and he doubted she considered him at all.

But still Delacourt scowled. "I apologize again for having to leave you. Please, allow me escort you to supper, Marianne," he said in a pinched tone as he stepped closer and held out an arm to his sister.

It was only then that Sebastian realized he was still holding her hand. With a quick inhale of breath, he released her and she stepped toward her brother, oblivious to the undercurrent of Delacourt's displeasure, just as she always had been.

But as Delacourt escorted her toward the dining room, she half-turned and sent Sebastian a grateful smile.

Sebastian felt a swell of uncommon emotion in his chest at the expression. Of pride that he had helped her in a moment of heart-break. And a warmth toward her that he had never allowed for any other woman, because he had never called another something so dear as "friend".

If he had it his way, that would never change.

CHAPTER 2

Marianne sat at her dressing table, hair down around her waist, robe tied tightly to keep out the night's chill, and stared at the box wrapped in plain brown paper in front of her. She had returned home from a surprisingly pleasant supper at her brother's, thanks mostly to Sebastian and his attempts to raise her spirits, to find that Claudia's brother had been true to his word. Her friend's final gift to her had been sent over while Marianne was out.

And now she just stared at the paper-wrapped parcel, reluctant to open it or even touch it for fear that doing so would only cause a return of the intense grief that had been briefly chased away by good company.

Finally she reached out and picked it up. With trembling fingers, she used a letter opener on her table to cut the string that had bound it for its transport. It fell away to the floor, forgotten before it even hit the wooden surface. She tossed the paper aside just as carelessly and then sucked in her breath.

The jewelry box was as beautiful as she had remembered. Intricately carved from the finest rosewood, it had then been inlaid with brass along the edges. The metal had been cut in exquisite curves and swirls. Finally, an ethereal and rather lonely image of a lady in the midst of her toilette had been painted on the top of the lid. There was a lock at the seam on the front and from it two small keys dangled, one fitted into the lock, the other free.

"Oh, Claudia," Marianne sighed as she set the box back down on the dressing table and stared at it.

As the marquess had done, Claudia had also mentioned before that her maiden aunt had given her the jewelry box. Unlike Claudia and Marianne, the aunt had been an eccentric and adventurous spinster, who traveled the world and had even been whispered to have scandalous affairs. Perhaps that's where Claudia had gotten her occasional whispered dreams of adventure and independence.

Marianne knew how much the gift had meant to Claudia.

"I will cherish this," she promised her friend's spirit. "And think of you always when I look at it or use it."

She smiled past her tears and reached out to turn the little key already in the lock. The top opened and she set the keys aside as she looked inside where velvet lined the spaces for rings or necklaces or bracelets. She had little jewelry, but what she did have would fit.

She opened the drawer of her table and drew out a few precious items to place inside, but as she set the first ring into a snug little pocket designed for it, she noticed something peculiar. There was a slight imperfection in the velvet along the back of the box.

Setting the ring aside temporarily, Marianne drew the container to the edge of her table and leaned closer. There was definitely something wrong with the velvet. She touched it and felt something beneath the fine fabric. It was flat, like a folded sheet of paper.

But that couldn't be correct, for it made no sense whatsoever.

She felt along the seam between the main compartment of the box and the backing, but it seemed firmly attached. There was no way someone could have slipped something behind the backing without damaging the velvet, and yet it remained unmarred.

"How very odd," Marianne murmured to herself as she slid her candle closer to inspect the fabric even more carefully. "How in the world would it get there? And more importantly, what in the world is it?"

She lifted the chest and looked at it, slowly turning it until the back faced her. She had never seen the box anywhere but in its place on her friend's table and had not thought to lift it or paw at it, so she had never known that the beautiful brass filigrees crisscrossed all along the back of the box.

"Lovely," she breathed, briefly forgetting the secret stuffed behind the velvet as she examined the delicate lattice work of the brass in the light of her candle.

And that was when she saw it. Hidden within the intricate decoration along the back, so well incorporated that one would never see it until one was looking for it, was another keyhole.

"The second key," she whispered as she snatched the set from the table where she had placed them after a few moments earlier. She fumbled with the two, first trying the wrong key, but finally the correct one slipped into the second lock and there was a faint click as the mechanism opened and the entire backing of the container went loose.

Heart pounding at the unexpected mystery of it all, Marianne gently set the wooden backing aside and slid her candle to the correct angle to see what was hidden within. There, propped up in a narrow secret chamber, was a folded piece of heavy vellum paper. It had been carefully tied with a crimson ribbon and set into the space.

Her hands shook as she drew it out. As she set the box back onto the table, she stared at the folded paper. Should she open it? The jewelry container had been given to her, to be certain, but the marquess had said nothing about a hidden note. Likely he hadn't even known about it. This item, whatever it was, wasn't something the average person was meant to find.

But perhaps her friend *had* wanted her to find it. Perhaps the note was the real gift, not the item which contained it. And if she simply burned it to protect Claudia's privacy, it might be against her friend's wishes.

"Bother," Marianne muttered, and then carefully loosened the ribbon around the paper. She unfolded it and sucked in a breath. It was written in Claudia's hand. Even, fine swirls of words that were far more elegant than Marianne's messier scratch. She had always envied Claudia's fine script.

She shook her head and read the words before her. It was not a note, a final farewell, as she had expected and even hoped for. Instead it was...a list.

Daring to Live Before I Die, Things to Do was written across the top, and Marianne choked on a sob as she read the date. Claudia had written this list the day after she had suddenly fallen ill.

Marianne turned her attention to the list itself and her mouth fell open. Dear Lord, her friend hadn't been exaggerating when she called her list daring. The items before her were that and more:

Learn What Naughty Words Mean and Use Them in a Proper Sentence.

Marianne stared at the first item, reading it over and over. Claudia couldn't have been serious to want to know this. Even less so to actually want to use those words out loud. Of course...Marianne had always wondered about those words, too. Sometimes when she overheard her brother and his friends saying certain things, she'd been very curious.

Go to a Party Uninvited.

Why, the very idea was terrifying! A person would be swiftly found out and judged and talked about. No one wanted that.

Get Drunk.

Again, she couldn't picture a scenario where that would be a good idea. She rarely drank at all, just a little madeira from time to time, or a sherry after supper if there was nothing else to find. But to get fully drunk? That would imply a loss of control she wasn't certain she desired.

Sneak Into a Gentleman's Home.

"Claudia!" she gasped, as if to admonish a dead woman.

Say Something Shocking.

As if her friend hadn't already said...or at least written, all these shocking things. She'd known Claudia sometimes longed for more adventure, but never that she'd gone so far as to imagine these kinds of scenarios.

Wear Something Daring.

Marianne's hand came up to touch the modest neckline of her own nightgown, almost out of habit.

Learn to Play Billiards.

At their annual country retreat just outside of London, she'd often seen or heard her brother and his friends playing billiards. It seemed a very loud game. Bending over the table couldn't be comfortable.

Be Unchaperoned with a Man.

Marianne pursed her lips. Aside from her brother, the only man Marianne was alone with on rare occasion was Sebastian and she doubted that a pleasant conversation with the door open was what Claudia had meant.

Fill My Dance Card.

"We were wallflowers," Marianne muttered. "How did you intend to pull that off?"

Find Out What Boxing is All About.

Boxing! Great Lord. It wasn't that she hadn't heard of the rare female fighter. They were somewhat of a rage right now, with shocking announcements about their fights put in the paper from time to time. But she knew their exhibitions weren't seen to be fit for a lady's eyes. The idea of coming into a...a ring? Wasn't it called a ring? Well, whatever it was, then swinging around trying to hit people? It was nearly enough to make a lady faint dead away.

Experience a Perfect Kiss.

There Marianne paused and her heart began to throb. As much as she wanted to dismiss these things as wild and unbelievable to desire, this one hit her in a much deeper place. A perfect kiss. Oh, hadn't she dreamed of those. Fantasized about being the kind of woman who would experience such a thing.

Play Faro in a Hell.

She and Claudia had loved to play cards together, so she supposed she understood the draw with that one. A hell had to be different than playing a friendly game with low stakes with other ladies, though.

Have a Love Affair.

She shivered at the idea. A love affair implied something outside the bounds of a marriage. Had Claudia truly dreamed of something so scandalous? And why did it make Marianne tingle all over when she imagined the same?

That was all the list, thank goodness.

"What in the world were you thinking, Claudia?" she whispered to herself as she stood with the paper in hand and paced to the fire.

She stood there, staring at the list and then the flames. Part of her said that Claudia had written this inventory of shocking things to do in a moment that was probably the height of her desperation. She had been ill, close to dying, though she had hidden that fact from Marianne for almost a week before admitting how serious her condition was. This list was nothing more than a fantasy of a troubled mind and burning it was a kindness so that no one else would find it somehow and judge Claudia as frivolous or foolish for her wild thoughts.

But there was another part that kept the list in her hand instead of in the flames. A part of Marianne that kept remembering the scant few uncaring souls who had bothered to come to her friend's funeral. People who would likely not even remember her in a few months' time. And why? Because Claudia had never done any of the things on her list. Claudia had followed the rules, always and forever.

Just like Marianne did.

They had both been labeled spinsters, though for different reasons. Claudia had come out during a Season with several of the most beautiful women in Society. Everyone had flocked to them and Claudia's painful shyness and lack of confidence with people she didn't know well hadn't helped. No one got to know her as well as Marianne had, so a few years had gone by without offers and suddenly Claudia had found herself a wallflower.

For Marianne, her fall had been far more painful and immediate. Her mother's spiral into emotional overwhelm and eventual death the year before her coming out had darkened her first Season. And then there was her father, who had blamed and shouted and forced her into an even worse second one before he, too, succumbed to his final end.

Marianne had never had any chance on the marriage mart.

Thankfully, though, she had met Claudia and together they had stood on the edge of dancefloors, smiling politely as everyone else had a glorious time. They had ignored any catty remarks of the Diamonds of the First Water and accepted that this was the life they would lead until they were elderly like her maiden aunt Beulah.

Or at least, *Marianne* had.

It seemed Claudia had dared to think of something different. Marianne knew that, of course, they'd spoken of it. But she'd taken it so far as to write these things down, to make them more than a mere conversation that disappeared on the wind.

She'd truly thought about taking the expectations of everyone around them and setting them aside to *live* before she died, just as the title of her list said. Only her friend hadn't been able to do any of it. Her disease had progressed too swiftly and her list had remained hidden in a jewelry box, yet another unfulfilled dream in a long string of unfulfilled dreams.

If Marianne destroyed it, she would be erasing those dreams forever. Locking them away until they became regrets. And Lord knew she would likely have enough of those before her own time came.

She stared once more at the account of things to do. She never would have thought of any of them, but now that she saw them and the initial shock began to wear off…she found something else was left in its wake. She read the list again and was tempted. Seduced.

"What would the harm be?" she whispered as she drew away from the fire almost without realizing she was doing it. "To do a *few* things on this list. For Claudia?"

The moment the words escaped her lips, heat flooded Marianne's cheeks. What in the world was she thinking? Obviously her grief and exhaustion had gotten the better of her. She had a place in life. And it wasn't to *fill her dance card* or *attend a party uninvited*, as her friend had written on her "Things To Do" inventory.

She would do better to remember that and simply bring flowers to Claudia's grave each week.

With that she shoved the list rather violently back into its hiding place, fumbled to replace the backing on the jewelry box and locked it. Then she went to her bed, blew out the candle and threw herself under the covers.

But sleep did not come easy. And when it did, it was filled with thoughts of confronting enemies and entering into scandalous affairs. Of being bold and daring and changing her life…for better or for worse.

The next morning, as Marianne sat at the breakfast table on the veranda in the morning sunshine, her thoughts continued to turn, against her will, toward her friend's damnable list. When she had readied herself for the day, it seemed the jewelry box mocked her from her dressing table, reminding her both of its secret and her own cowardice.

Before she could work herself into too much of a tizzy, her aunt Beulah stepped out onto the veranda and settled her frail frame onto the seat across from her.

"Good morning, my dear," she said with a warm and genuine smile.

"Good morning, Auntie," Marianne said, doing her best not to sound as absent as she felt.

It was an unusual arrangement that she shared with her aunt, but one she truly enjoyed. As an unmarried woman, Marianne would normally be expected to remain in her brother's home under the never-ending protection of his watchful eye. But as it became more and more clear that she would likely never marry, she had been able to convince Finn, with much effort, that she could live very pleasantly in a townhouse with their great-aunt as chaperone.

Her dutiful brother *had* argued against it for a while, but in the end...well, though he tried to act properly when she was around, Marianne had no illusions that he lived as a choir boy or monk. Without a spinster sister in the house he had afforded himself as much increased freedom as he had given her. Finn gave her a generous living and she didn't have to answer to anyone about where she went or who she saw.

Except for Aunt Beulah, who often did not pay attention. After all, it wasn't as if Marianne was getting into any trouble.

And her mind turned treacherously to that blasted list once more.

"You look tired, my dear," her aunt said as she sipped her tea. "Did you not sleep well?"

Marianne blinked in surprise at her aunt's observation. "N-No, I'm afraid I didn't. Thoughts of Claudia kept me awake."

Which was true, though not only in the way her aunt would assume.

Beulah's mouth drew down in sadness. "Ah yes. It is hard to lose a friend, especially at so young an age. I have lost a great many in the past few years, but then I am nearly eighty and at a point where I expect such things."

Marianne nodded slowly. Yes, her aunt *had* lost a few companions from her group as her age advanced. She had escorted Beulah to many of the funerals...and as with Claudia, there were few mourners for spinsters. Those who came did not seem to grieve overly much. Occasionally a favorite niece would cry or a sibling would seem touched by their loss, but for the most part there was often a sense of...relief. Like the deceased was a troubling obligation better left undone.

Marianne set her tea aside and shook her head. "Have you ever wished..." She trailed off.

Her aunt's eyes came up and she looked at Marianne sharply. "Wished?"

"Nothing," Marianne said with blush. It was too humiliating to say out loud.

"No," her aunt pressed as she leaned closer. "You wanted to ask me something. I'd like to hear it."

Marianne shifted uncomfortably. Though she liked her aunt and didn't mind sharing a home with her, they had not ever had deep discussions. Certainly, they'd never aired their thoughts on their shared lot in life.

"Haven't you ever wished for...more?" Marianne whispered. "More than just being—"

"An old maid?" her aunt asked, and then broke into a surprising burst of laughter. "Of course, my dear. Do you think any girl dreams of being alone, living on the charity of family until her death where hardly a soul will mourn?"

Marianne flinched, but her aunt seemed oblivious to the fact that she had touched upon her niece's very heartache. "No, I suppose not," Marianne said with a sigh.

"At one time, I wished for children and marriage, even something so foolish as love." Her aunt shrugged. "But after a time, I came to realize that these things were never meant for me. Now you..." She smiled and it was warm. "*You* could still have a chance."

"Oh, I don't think so." Marianne shook her head.

Her aunt took a sip from her cup. "Your debut and the years following it were disastrous, I know. Your mother's passing and the things that preceded it—"

Her aunt stopped and Marianne looked at the table with as

much focus as she could manage. Her mother had always been an emotional person. Her father would often hiss about her hysteria, though Marianne had never felt it went that far until the horrible series of events that led to her untimely death. She flinched just thinking of it and pushed those thoughts aside so that they didn't overwhelm her.

Still, by the end of her debut year, the damage was done, both personally and in Marianne's fruitless search for a groom. It was only her late father's good name and her brother's calm handling of the entire situation that allowed her continued invitation to any events even now.

"Well, let's just say the deaths of your parents," her aunt finished softly. "Those things were out of your control. But a nice widower looking for a mother for his children might very well be the perfect fit for you. It's been long enough that he could very well overlook the past. And there is nothing wrong in settling."

Marianne stiffened as she took up her cup. "So it is to settle for someone who cares nothing for me, but is willing to overlook my… *spinsterhood*…or to accept that for the next perhaps fifty years my life will play out just as it is at this moment?"

Her aunt blinked in confusion at the question. "There are no other choices, are there?"

Once again Marianne's thoughts returned to that list. She could almost see each item in her mind. Taunting her with another choice. A choice to *live*!

After all, if her ultimate existence was to be one of loneliness, why shouldn't she experience something first? What was the worst that could happen? Societal shunning? She was hardly accepted in society as it was. The loss would not be a great one…

"Oh dear." Her aunt reached out and covered her hand. "I do not say this to hurt you. Only that you asked me my thoughts. And I believe that the sooner we simply accept what we are and what our place is, the more content we will eventually be with that place. Over time, the sting eases, I assure you."

Marianne smiled at her aunt, for she knew Beulah truly didn't mean to hurt her. But as they each returned to their breakfast, Marianne couldn't help but steal a glance at her. What she described as quiet acceptance of a circumstance she could not change, Marianne presently saw as surrender to despair.

And worse, when she looked at her aunt, she saw her own future ten, twenty, thirty years down the road. There was no reason to think her life would end any differently than Beulah's would...or Claudia's had.

And that left her once again with thoughts of her friend's unfinished list. Her unfinished dreams of something more interesting than surrender. Of experiencing life.

Marianne's expression did not change. She made certain of it, for she didn't want to face questions in case her aunt noticed. But deep within her, she felt that *she* had changed. Because Great-Aunt Beulah might not have meant to do so, but she had driven Marianne to a choice.

She was going to complete as many of the items on Claudia's abandoned list as she could, no matter how utterly terrifying she found them. For her friend.

And for herself.

CHAPTER 3

When Marianne and Delacourt arrived at his home for a
drink before they all left for a ball, Sebastian could see that
Marianne was distracted. Thankfully, she had not worn another
unflattering black gown, but she still had a band of black around
her upper arm, rather like one would see a man wear after a loss.

If he hadn't known his friend so well, he might have simply
dismissed her unease as a reaction to Lady Claudia's death and left
it at that. But he *did* know Marianne and he was certain that there
was more to the way her gaze went distant and her attempts to add
to the conversation were so few. More strangely, he actually found
himself curious about the cause of her distress. An odd and unexpected sensation, indeed, for a man who always did his level best to
stay out of anything that required emotion or a deeper connection.

"Tonight's fete at Lady Simpson's should be a laugh, don't you
think?" he asked, keeping his eye on Marianne for her reaction.

She only blinked, her expression still distant, but her brother
answered instead.

"Why a laugh? I've always found her gatherings to be so boring."
Delacourt shuddered. "If her husband was not an important
member of parliament, I doubt anyone would go and drink her

watered-down spirits and listen to those horrible orchestras she has hired over the years. The woman must be completely unable to discern one note from another. Dear Lord, the last one practically picked their way through the waltz."

"And *that* is why it is a laugh, Delacourt," Sebastian chuckled. "Don't you think, Marianne?"

She shook her head and turned toward him. She was pale and for the first time he noted just the faintest of shadows beneath her eyes. Yes, something was definitely troubling her.

"I'm sorry, I was woolgathering. What are we discussing?" she asked with a deep blush.

Sebastian arched a playful brow. "The fact that the disastrous qualities of poor Lady Simpson's balls are the reason they are so entertaining. Would you not agree?"

For the first time that night, Marianne smiled. It was a faint shadow of her usual expression, but it was there and a swell of pride filled Sebastian. "I do agree."

"You two are clearly troubled if you think standing through her wretched gatherings is an entertainment," Delacourt said as he set his empty drink aside with a shake of his head. "Come, let's go to the carriage."

Sebastian offered Marianne an arm before her brother could, and though Delacourt's posture stiffened, he said nothing as he led them from the room to the waiting vehicle. They would travel together, but Sebastian's own driver would follow shortly so that he could leave when…and with whom…he desired.

He helped Marianne into the rig and after they were all settled and the carriage began to roll the short distance to Lord and Lady Simpson's residence, he tilted his head. "Your brother may not share our amusement at the massive failure of poor Lady Simpson's gatherings, but perhaps if we made it into a game that would change his mind."

Delacourt looked at him with suspicion. "A game?"

Marianne was also staring across the expanse between them, but her eyes had gone a bit wider with interest. "Yes, Sebastian, what kind of game could we possibly play?"

He lifted a finger to his lips. "Each time Lady Simpson introduces two people who despise each other, we must tilt our glasses in salute. And when she boasts too loudly about the cost of the gathering, we must take a sip."

Marianne laughed. "Oh, I like this. What about when the orchestra plays poorly? Or goes off time and makes the dancers nearly crash headlong into each other?"

"A drink full-on, my dear," Sebastian laughed. "What else would it be?"

The carriage pulled to a stop and Delacourt let out a very put-upon and rather theatrical sigh. "You are both a menace to Society at large. I refuse to participate in these childish diversions. If you two wish to make a spectacle of yourselves, then leave me out of it."

Marianne turned to look out the window away from her brother, but Sebastian caught her expression before shadow overtook her features. His words seemed to make her highly uncomfortable, even though he didn't think Delacourt meant them harshly.

He kept his gaze on her as he said, "Great God, Delacourt, you are a bore. He only does this because of you, Marianne."

She turned back toward them with a gasp, but it turned to a smile as she took his meaning. "Ah, you mean because Finn thinks I am a delicate flower who must be protected at all costs from anything daring or, Lord preserve us, *fun.*"

Delacourt rolled his eyes, but Sebastian could see he was trying not to smile. Although his friend tended to be serious and dry at these events, he would wager Delacourt actually enjoyed his shenanigans. Otherwise, they couldn't have remained friends for so long. "Again, I fail to see how this…punch-drinking game of yours will be fun."

Sebastian let out a long and put-upon sigh. "*Fine,* if you are determined to play the staid lord of the manor, then you are no longer invited to take part in the game. Marianne and I shall play without you, won't we, my lady?"

For a moment her face paled, and when she finally answered him, her mouth was firm in a line of determination rather than amusement. "Yes," she said with far more passion than the subject demanded.

If Delacourt noticed her change in demeanor, he didn't acknowledge it, just threw the carriage door open with an exaggerated groan of disapproval and stepped out. As he helped Marianne out and the two moved out of the way so that Sebastian could come outside, he couldn't help but stare at Marianne. She had always been a friend in his eyes, but never had he been so interested in her motives. But there was something going on with her and he was going to find out what that something was.

One way or another.

Marianne stood on the veranda overlooking a pretty garden below. She clung to the edge of the stone with both hands as the world tilted precariously about her and tried not to pitch headfirst into the bushes down below.

"There you are."

Marianne sucked in a long breath of fresh, cool air and then slowly turned to find Sebastian standing at the doors of the veranda. It boded poorly for her that he had two drinks in his hands.

"You missed three ladies tumbling into each other in a spectacular crash on the dance floor thanks to the orchestra changing its tune right in the middle of one of the country jigs." Sebastian moved closer and handed her a glass. "So this is for you."

Marianne took the glass and swallowed hard as she stared at the liquid within. But she had made a promise and all she could do was take a large sip. As it made its way down her throat, she made a face.

"I am not feeling quite right," she admitted. Her voice seemed far away in her ears.

Sebastian looked at her for a moment and then reached out to take her elbow. "Well, the party was a stunning success for our game, though not for Lady Simpson."

He smiled and Marianne found herself staring at his mouth. It was such a nice mouth. Such a beautiful, kissable mouth.

Sebastian, apparently oblivious to her shocking thoughts, moved her toward some benches farther back in the shadow of the terrace. "Dear Lord, you're drunk, aren't you?"

Marianne blinked. "Am I? Is this what being drunk feels like?"

Sebastian chuckled low in the dark and the sound of it sent a tingle down Marianne's spine that she had never experienced before. "Is the world spinning?"

Marianne nodded and the movement proved Sebastian's point exactly. "Yes."

"Do you feel out of control? Foggy?"

"Most definitely," she said.

"And you're slurring your words slightly," he mused, though it seemed like he was saying it more to himself than to her.

"I am not," Marianne protested, indignation rising up in her. "I sh-sound perfectly fine."

"Yes, I believe you are at least a bit tipsy," Sebastian laughed again. "I should apologize. I wasn't thinking that this would be the outcome when I proposed our game, but between the fact that you rarely drink and that Lady Simpson made some particularly grue-some faux pas tonight, it might not have been the best time to play."

Marianne nodded, but the movement only made her head spin again. "Drunk. Well, that's nice. I can cross that off the list."

Sebastian looked at her in confusion. "List?"

Marianne stared up at him. The moon cast the only light in this dark corner and it partially illuminated his face in a most interesting way. What was he asking about? The list? But he didn't know about the list. No one knew.

But he could help her. Lord knew he had experience in some shocking things. He was the perfect person to assist her with a few of the items Claudia had wanted to do before her death.

"Do you think you could teach me some naughty words?" Marianne asked.

Sebastian had taken another sip of his drink and he began to choke on it. He drew out a handkerchief and coughed into it for a moment before he gathered his composure.

"Naughty words?" he repeated in blank disbelief.

Marianne nodded. "Yes. I'd like to know how to ush...use them. Like..." She searched the foggy annals of her mind for words she had heard men on the street use, or her brother if he thought she wasn't nearby. "Like *bollocks* and *doxy* and—"

Before she could say more, Sebastian reached out and covered her hand with his. It felt so warm and heavy. Comforting. Why was her body tingling?

"Yes, yes," he said. "I-I understand. But why—" He cut himself off with a laugh and a shake of his head. "Actually, I'm not certain you're in much condition to even know *why* you would want to know such things. But I shall come by to see you tomorrow and we can discuss it in private when your mind is clearer."

"My mind," Marianne hiccuped, "is perfectly clear."

Sebastian stared at her a moment and then he reached up and gently tucked a strand of hair behind her ear. It was a delicate gesture and Marianne's heart began to pound at it.

"Of course it is," he said softly. Then he shook his head. "Now we shall find your brother. I'll tell him that you have a headache and need to go home. If you remain quiet, there is no reason he needs know that you are at least somewhat in your cups, do you understand?"

Marianne smiled. Good, so she would know the naughty words. That would be two items off her list in just a day's time. Excellent.

"Marianne?" he repeated. "Do you understand?"

She nodded. "Yes, Shebas…Sebastian. Of course. I shall be quiet as a church moushe. I've had plenty of practice at that."

Sebastian looked at her. Even in her fog, even in the dim light, she saw the troubled expression on his face, and the surprise in his eyes when she said that. Then he nodded.

"Yes, I suppose you have." Then the trouble was gone and he smiled as he got to his feet and offered her an arm. "Come, my lady. I shall make certain you arrive home safely."

Marianne took his offering and leaned on him slightly as he maneuvered her toward the door. "Thank you. And don't forget, you promised me. You promised you would help me."

"Yes. I did. And I keep my promises."

CHAPTER 4

Sebastian was careful to wait until mid-afternoon to arrive at Marianne's home on St. James Street. After the previous night, he would hazard a guess that she was still feeling the effects of too much drink. Hopefully she'd had a chance to sleep it all off.

And now he stood in her front parlor, staring around the room, shocked by the fact that he didn't think he'd ever come to her home before. He always met her at Delacourt's estate a mile away, or at his own. And Delacourt was always in attendance at those times so they were never alone for more than a few moments at a time. But he doubted his friend was here now, not with her asking for such shocking help from Sebastian.

So the whole exercise felt…odd. Odder still was the fussy parlor. It was truly the domain of a spinster with its doilies and miniatures of elderly relatives. It didn't feel like Marianne. Despite her labeling by Society as such, she never seemed like a spinster to Sebastian. Not truly. No, Marianne was in a category all her own.

The door behind him opened and he turned to watch her enter the chamber. Her dark hair and gown were impeccable, and if one only looked that far, she would be the perfect vision of a lady.

However, her cheeks were pale and her eyes a little glassy. He smiled slightly. It seemed she *was* still hungover.

"Sebastian," she said as she slowly advanced on him, hand outstretched in welcome. "I didn't expect you."

He lifted her knuckles to his lips briefly and laughed at her as he released her. "My God, you really were in your cups. You must be miserable."

Now color rushed to those pale cheeks and she took a few wobbly steps to the settee, where she sank down. "I am," she admitted. "My head throbs and I'm certain I'll cast up my accounts at any moment."

He shook his head slowly, both amused by her and also driven to help. "That will not do at all. One moment."

He crossed to the door and rang the bell. In a few moments her butler appeared. "May I help you, my lord?"

Sebastian leaned forward and quietly requested a few items from the servant. It seemed the old man might refuse, but when he looked past Sebastian to Marianne, worry for his mistress overrode whatever hesitations he had at being ordered around by a stranger, even a titled one.

"Yes, my lord. Immediately."

Sebastian nodded and then turned back to Marianne. She was staring at him. "Oh, what in the world did you ask Adams for?"

"You'll see. Nothing terrible, I promise you."

She covered her face with her hands. "I'm so embarrassed that my staff has seen me in such a state. I'm sure they're all whispering below stairs."

He moved to her and sat momentarily, catching her hand again. She wasn't wearing gloves and her palm was soft in his. "My dear Marianne, you are not the first person to have a few too many drinks at a spirited gathering. You won't be the last. And I'm certain that you were charming and kind to your staff, as you always are to everyone, whatever state you're in. I know you were so when we were on the veranda together last night."

34

"We were on the veranda?" she gasped.

He laughed again, but before he could say anything the butler returned with the items Sebastian had suggested, which he set up along the sideboard. When he had gone, Sebastian went to them and took up a crystal glass from a set. He went to work, feeling Marianne watching his every move, even if he didn't look at her.

When he returned, holding out the glass that was now filled with cloudy liquid, she eyed it suspiciously. "What's floating in it?" she asked.

"It's better not to know," he assured her. "Just drink up."

"I trust you," she said softly, and then took a large swig of the liquid before he could fully digest those words. She gasped and coughed, glaring at him over the rim of the glass. "Sebastian, that is dreadful!"

He nodded. "It is, it really is. But it *will* help. I am far too experienced at recovering from overindulgences, I'm afraid. Terrible character flaw, but it allows me to be your servant in this case. Keep drinking and let's discuss why it was you invited me here today."

Her eyes went wide as she struggled to swallow a second mouthful of the curative. "I invited you?" she said at last. "Good Lord, I *was* senseless, it seems."

He laughed softly. "A bit. And yes, you invited me. You said you wanted my help. You were *desperate* for it."

She took the last sip of the drink and set the empty glass aside with a disgusted expression. "I think you're teasing me."

"*Me?*" he said with a shake of his head. "You wound me. I would never."

She smiled a little and he once again felt that triumph that he could cause it. It was always fun to play with her, tease her gently, watch her blush and titter. "Help me with what, exactly? Or did I say in this altered state you describe?"

"Well," he said with a wink. "You said you wanted to learn some naughty words. You said something about a list."

Her lips parted and now the teasing pleasure left her face as she got to her feet and swayed slightly. Then she took a long step away, putting her back to him. "A-a list? Whatever could that mean?"

He wrinkled his brow. *That* was an interesting response. Almost…guilty. Fascinating. It only made him want to understand more about why.

He pushed to his feet and took a long step toward her, crowding into the space she had created by walking away. "I'm sure I couldn't know. Perhaps we could talk it out. Try to get to the bottom of it together."

She pivoted and seemed surprised by his proximity if the way she jolted as she looked up into his face was any indication. "I'm certain it was just a strange twist of phrase in my drunken state. It needs no—no further exploration."

He narrowed his eyes as he examined her. She was trembling ever so slightly. "I see. So does that mean you don't want to learn any swear words, *naughty words* as you put it?"

Briefly panic crossed her face at the idea that he would leave, but then she smoothed it away. He tilted his head at how good at covering her emotions she was. Had she always been so?

"Well…well, you kindly came all the way here to call for the purpose didn't you?" she asked. "It seems rude if I turned you away instead of taking you up on the offer."

He nodded slowly, but he was gathering evidence as he did so. It seemed that though she might not remember entirely what had happened the night before, she knew *exactly* why she'd asked to learn profanities from him. She still wanted to know them, even if she would deny him the true reason why.

He stepped closer and now he was near enough that he could reach out to touch her. He heard her breath catch, watched as her pupils dilated ever so slightly when he moved into her space.

But she didn't back away, not even when he said, "Do you want to tell me what's really going on, Marianne?"

~

The world was spinning as Marianne stared up into the brightest, bluest eyes she'd ever seen and found them so entirely focused on her that she could hardly draw breath. Sebastian had always paid her attention, of course, but it was playful. And though this…interrogation, for she had no better word for it…had begun that way, now it felt like it had shifted. The entire world had shifted actually, and her knees were trembling as she tried to gather her wits.

He wanted to know what she was doing, why she was asking him for such inappropriate things, but she couldn't tell him. Not him. He would pity her for one. And he would most definitely report her actions to Finn. Her brother would never understand. Never. He might even try to stop her in some misguided attempt at protection.

"Going on?" she whispered, and then cleared her throat to try to make her voice stronger. "I cannot imagine what you mean."

"Marianne," he said, and it felt like his voice got deeper when he put that warning edge to it. Like it resonated all the way down her spine.

Despite all the good reasons she had just listed to herself not to tell him, in that moment she almost wished to ignore all that and do it. Give him her heartbreak and her desire to be more than just a pathetic wallflower that no one thought of, if only for a few short days or weeks.

But no.

"I promise you, Sebastian, there is nothing going on beyond my utter and complete boredom. And since you came here today, that must mean you agreed to teach me about swear words."

He pursed his lips and for a moment she thought he might force her hand. But then he shook his head and the teasing light returned to his eyes. He let out a small sigh before he said, "Of course I agreed, Marianne. How could I ever resist you? I'll do as you ask if you still desire it while stone-cold sober. Certainly I think it will be entertaining to hear wicked things coming from that sweet mouth of yours."

His gaze slipped from her own and hovered for a moment on her lips. And once again the mood in the room shifted. But this time it wasn't fraught with danger but something else. Something heated. She felt tingly as his eyes lingered on her mouth, discombobulated just as she had when she'd been in her cups.

He blinked and his gaze darted away from her entirely. "Are you...are you concerned that we might be interrupted by your aunt in this wicked exercise?"

She shook her head. "No. Aunt Beulah is making calls to friends today. She won't be back for ages."

His breath shortened and he paced away, pointing to a chair before the fire as he did so. "Sit," he ordered.

She swallowed, trying to push away all these odd feelings and did as she had been told. He made no effort to do the same, but crossed back to the sideboard and poured himself a drink. She rubbed suddenly sweaty palms on her gown as he did so and waited.

At last, he turned back and all the heat she had felt from him was gone. Her friend was back, mischief in his stare, a grin quirking his full lips. The rest she must have imagined, there was no other explanation.

"Do you know of a bobtail, my fair lady?" he asked.

She shook her head. "I've never heard the term."

He smiled slightly. "Why, it's the term for a lewd woman."

She felt her eyes widen and his smile did the same. "A bobtail, gracious," she said. "A lewd woman would be...what would one do to be considered lewd?"

His smile faltered a bit. "Er, well, one who is lasciviously interested in sex, I suppose. One who fucks without thought of consequence." He arched a brow.

She flinched. "I've heard my brother say 'fuck' before, but never when he knew I was near. Is that a term for...for marital relations?"

"Not only marital," he said. "There are many a couple who indulge in conjugal pleasures without wedlock."

"I suppose there are," she said, feeling her cheeks heat with the bold nature of this conversation. She hadn't really thought through the fact that discussing dirty words would also involve discussing their meaning. "Does that...does that mean that *you* are considered a lewd gentleman?"

Now it was his eyes that widened and he took a long swig of his drink before he answered. "In some circles I must be known as such, yes. Unfairly, men are not held to the same standards as woman, especially in our class. To be a rake does not necessarily mean to be held in lower regard."

She pursed her lips. "But it *is* very different for women, yes. We're taught to not even have such desires in our minds, let alone act on them."

His brow wrinkled. "Having desires isn't wrong, Marianne. It's human. No matter what anyone teaches you. And no one has to know what is in your head, do they?"

"I suppose not," she said, and thought of Claudia's list, locked up in her chamber at present. "Perhaps that's for the best."

He leaned back. "Does that mean Lady Marianne has a secret, rich fantasy life?"

She shook her head. "Oh...oh no. Of course not. I couldn't...I wouldn't even know what to imagine."

"That's a shame," he said, taking a step toward her before he stopped himself. "Fantasy makes reality worthwhile sometimes."

Her mind floated, quite of its own accord, to foggy dreams she sometimes had of the very man before her. Of his gaze holding hers as it was now, of him taking her hand. Of him kissing her. She felt the heat on her cheeks increase as she turned away. "What other words are there?"

He hesitated a moment before he said, "A man's member is called a cock."

She pivoted back to him. "Like a male chicken!"

He laughed at her expression and once again the tension in the room faded a fraction. "Indeed."

"Why in the world would one call such a thing a cock?" she asked.

He swallowed hard and then shrugged one shoulder. "Well, when a man is...is excited by a woman...when he wants her, his cock stands up straight."

She sucked in a breath. She'd never been close to marriage, so she'd never had the conversations other women had to explain what to expect in the marital bed. It seemed she would learn a great deal more than just about swearing today. "It does?" she said. "Why?"

"Great God," he muttered beneath his breath and shifted before he took a seat on the settee across from her and crossed his legs. "Well, er...he wants to take the woman, you see. Have you...have you ever seen animals rut in the country?"

"I...yes," she said. "That is how it is with...with..." She dropped her voice. "Fucking?"

Once again he sucked in a breath. "Yes. Without the cock being hard, standing at attention, it would be difficult to put...it...inside. And I suppose the way a male chicken stands up straight and races around, certain and wild, is a bit similar." He cleared his throat. "Do you understand?"

"Not entirely, but I'll take your word for it." She clenched and unclenched her hands in her lap. "And what do you call a woman's...parts?"

"There are a great many words for that," he said, leaning forward. "Her dumb glutton."

"Oh." She pulled a face. "That isn't very nice."

"I agree. Not my favorite." He smiled slightly, but it was growing more wicked by the moment. "Her hat."

"What?" She shook her head. "Now you're just teasing me."

"I'm not!" he insisted. "They call it that because it is frequently felt."

Her mouth dropped open at the pun. "Sebastian!"

"I didn't create the term, nor the reason, my dear."

"It isn't fair. So a man gets a cock and a woman gets such odd terms?"

"Well, there are better ones. Her cunt, for example. Her pussy. Those are my preferred terms for such things."

There was something in the way he said those words that gave them more weight, more sensuality than the sillier names. She found herself shifting in her chair and the tingles between her legs increased when she did. She reached up to cover her hot cheeks with her cool hands. "It seems that most of the words are about… about…copulation."

He tilted his head as if to consider that. "I suppose that's true. As long as there has been language, there have been words to describe fucking."

"Why do you think that is?" she asked, trying to meet his eyes as if this was all normal instead of so odd and heated and strange a conversation.

"It is our basest instinct," he said without hesitation. "Our deepest pleasure that we try to pretend away in 'good' company. And yet it occupies our art, our language…and our dreams. Even if you don't admit it."

She dropped her gaze that he would bring her thoughts back around to her inappropriate dreams. "I suppose I have, from time to time, had an improper thought about a gentleman."

There was so long a silence that she forced herself to look at him. She found him staring at her intently. "Who?" he asked softly.

But before she could answer, he pushed to his feet and then turned away. "The afternoon grows late, I fear," he said. "And I think I've scandalized you enough for one day. I should go."

She blinked at the sudden formality to his tone and the way he moved stiffly when he walked across the room toward the door to the chamber. "I see. Of course, I wouldn't want to keep you," she said, making herself follow as a good hostess would. "Thank you for your help today. It was most educational."

"Excellent, I'm pleased to be of service."

He signaled to Adams for his horse to be brought and then turned to her. He was smiling, but there was something false about it. She'd never seen that kind of expression on his face, at least not when it came to her. She didn't like it.

"I hope you don't...don't judge me for asking," she said.

"No," he insisted. "Of course not. We'll see each other soon. Good day, Marianne."

And then he was gone, out her door and onto the stoop where he began to walk toward her small stable as if he couldn't wait for his animal to be brought. She shut the door slowly, confusion flooding her. But also a sense of excitement. Sebastian had opened her thoughts into a wide world she'd never been allowed to consider before in her sheltered life. So whatever happened next, at least she had been able to take a glimpse at that forbidden place of desire and sin.

Perhaps, if she continued down Claudia's path, she might even get a little more.

~

Sebastian mounted his horse and urged him forward, hastening to get himself out of Marianne's view as swiftly as possible.

What had he been thinking? It was one thing to playfully educate Marianne about the intricacies of inappropriate slang, but he'd gone further than he ever should. Not only had he only spoken to her about words that represented, as she had put it, copulation, but he had leaned into her. He'd drawn her out. Flirted the way he would with a woman he was actually pursuing.

And he'd seen her with different eyes because of it. When her lips had formed those filthy words, he had been physically affected. Even forced to block an erection from her view. Worse, he'd watched those lips and wondered what they would feel like pressed to his. What they would look like parted as she arched her back beneath a man.

Not just any man. Beneath him.

And he couldn't do those things with her. Delacourt had always been clear at the kind of boundaries that would need to be maintained in order to keep their friendship. So if he wanted to remain close to a man he considered brother, Sebastian would have to be more careful around Marianne.

That was all there was to it.

CHAPTER 5

Marianne had started so well when she'd decided to complete at least some of Claudia's list. Within days she'd crossed off three items: *Get Drunk. Learn Naughty Words. Be Unchaperoned with a Man.*

Well, she wasn't entirely certain she could count the last one. After all, though they had been alone together in the very parlor where she now stood, Sebastian wasn't interested in her. He liked to tease and play, but that meant nothing to him. Whatever she had thought was happening the afternoon they'd shared discussing slang together, there couldn't have truly been heat between them. He could have anyone he wanted. She was likely seen as almost sexless to him.

She sighed and looked out the window where rain streaked down the pane and almost obliterated her view of the soggy park across the lane. In the week since that day, she had not made any progress on the list. She could practically feel herself fading back into the wallpaper like the ghost she feared she'd someday be.

At least she would be forced to get out into the world today. Finn was taking her to an afternoon tea at Lord and Lady Nettlebaum's. Their daughter, Arabella, had come out that year and they seemed to be making a concerted effort to ensure the young lady didn't end up in the same position Marianne was.

Briefly she wondered if that was why she was invited: as a warning. She sighed. It wouldn't be the first time someone had used Marianne's unmarried status to frighten their innocent debutante. Which was all the more reason to rededicate herself to the list as much as she could.

"Lord Delacourt, my lady," Adams intoned, and then stepped away so that Finn could enter the parlor.

She forced a smile as she crossed to him. He'd been frowning as he entered the room, but his face softened as she leaned up to kiss his cheek. "Good day, Finn," she said.

"Mari. That is a pretty color on you."

"Thank you." She examined his face a little closer. His expression was always hard—even as a boy he'd been very serious and difficult to read. When one managed to coax a smile from him, it felt all the better. "Are you well?" she asked.

"Of course," he said quickly. "Come, why don't we call for the carriage? I think we'll be just fashionably late to this affair if we start now."

"Oh yes, if you're fashionably late you'll make even more of a splash," she teased him gently.

He took her arm and they headed to where the carriage was already waiting. It seemed Finn had arranged it even before he joined her. She said a brief farewell to Adams and then let Finn help her into the carriage. Once she had settled into place and they'd begun to move, her brother speared her with a glance.

"Why would I want to make a splash?" he asked.

She laughed. "I'm certain you've been invited as a potential suitor for Lady Arabella," she said. "And you'll be the envy of all the men when you come in looking so handsome. Oh, but let me fix your cravat."

He leaned forward and allowed her to straighten him, but his frown deepened. "If Lady Arabella thinks I've any interest in her, she will be well disappointed. She's practically a child. I could not think of her any more than I'd think of a kitten."

She shook her head. "You'll have to marry at some point, Phineas."

She expected him to tease back, but his eyes narrowed and he sat back on the seat with a scowl. "I know that full-well, Marianne. I don't need advice on that score from you."

She flinched a little at the harshness of his statement. Finn never commented negatively on her status in life. Years ago he'd even given up encouraging her to seek suitors. He supported her and that was all, which made the comment all the sharper.

She cleared her throat slightly and decided to change the subject since this one made him so cross. "What did you do this morning before you came to collect me?"

His gaze flitted to her from the window and she could see his guilt at his previous words. He sighed. "It was a busy morning, in truth. I saw my solicitor about the Yorkshire estate."

"Oh, how was Mr. Richards? Is his wife recovered from her illness this past winter?"

His expression softened. "Always so kind, my dearest Marianne. Indeed, she's well. She's in London, in fact."

"Is she seeing the specialist you recommended?"

He nodded. "Yes, and before you ask, I'm paying the bill, just as you thought I should. I'm sure you could call on her and it would make her very happy. And after that, I went to my boxing club."

Marianne sat up a little straighter. *Find Out What Boxing is All About* was on Claudia's list and it brought Marianne right back to her duties in regards to the list.

"Oh," she said. "You know I've always been interested in that."

His brow wrinkled. "In what?"

She blushed a little at his entirely lost tone. "Boxing, silly. It seems a fascinating thing."

His jaw set a little. "It's a violent thing, Marianne. Not fit for a lady."

"Is it not?" she pressed. "I thought I had heard told of female boxing clubs in the city."

"There are those women who partake," he said slowly. "But they aren't...they aren't like you Marianne."

Now she drew back. After his earlier snide comment, she wasn't sure of his tone now. "What does that mean?"

He let out his breath in a long, put-upon sigh. "I've been going to my boxing club for years without you paying any mind to it. So why is this coming up now?"

That was an excellent question and one she had no intention of answering truthfully. So she had to invent a lie that would make sense. "I...I only thought that perhaps I need to know how to protect myself."

"From what?" he asked with a shake of his head. "Forgive me, but you aren't exactly running around London."

She folded her arms as her ire at his dismissiveness began to rise. "You think I couldn't. Or that no one would ever think of me beyond a boring spinster who wouldn't be worth troubling?"

As she said it, the words hit her and she felt like a balloon that had been deflated. It must have reflected on her face, for Finn reached across the carriage and touched her gloved hand briefly. "You aren't that."

She blinked at the sting of tears. "Of course I am," she said softly. "I'm sorry. I was just being silly asking you such things."

Finn opened his mouth like he wanted to say more, but the carriage slowed to a stop then and the doors were opened by the Nettlebaum staff. Marianne exited the vehicle first and Finn followed. He guided her to the door and through the greetings of their hosts, but he seemed distracted as he did. And once they entered the large parlor where the tea would be held, he gave her a small bow. "Forgive me, Marianne, I must excuse myself."

He left her without waiting for her response and she stood

staring after him, certain of her own reactions in the carriage, but confused about his. It seemed they each had their own secrets.

"Marianne."

She jumped at the sound of Sebastian's voice coming from just at her elbow. She turned to face him and covered her heart with her hand. "Gracious, you frightened me."

"Yes, you were very focused, brooding off into the distance," he teased. "I thought that was the purview of men."

"Hmmm, it seems a great deal is that," she said. "I'm surprised to see you here. I know you would be considered a catch by those like the Nettlebaums, but I cannot imagine you'd want to *be* caught by Arabella of all people."

He pulled a face. "She's comely enough, but no. Not a brain in her head, it seems. I danced with her a fortnight ago at a ball and all she talked about was bonnets. The fashions of bonnets. She's an expert on the subject and seemed to have no interest in any other I tried to press her on."

"Oh dear," Marianne said. "I'm guessing Arabella intends to get by on her looks and not her wit. Though she has a better chance using those tactics than I do talking endlessly about rise of the priestesses in the Roman empire or the latest book from Mr. Mattigan's shop. So perhaps she has the better of it."

"I'd much rather talk to you about priestesses," Sebastian said with a smile that felt far more real than the one she'd received from him last week. She was glad of it. When she hadn't seen him for so many days, she feared she'd spoiled their friendship with her forward desires for his help.

"You are the only one then," she said with a laugh.

He tilted his head and explored her face closer. "Is something wrong, Marianne?"

She blinked at him. She didn't feel like her upset was plain on her face, but somehow he could see it. She worried her lip slightly. "No. Yes. No."

"That's very confusing. Which one is it?" His tone was suddenly gentle.

She sighed. "I just had a bothersome conversation with Finn on the way here."

"About what?" Sebastian pressed even as she saw him scanning the crowd for her brother. Of course he would. He might not have known Finn would be here and he'd obviously want to go spend time with him over her.

"I suppose I cannot shock you any more than I already have in the last week or two," she said. "He mentioned he was at his boxing club today and I said I was interested in learning more." She swallowed because Sebastian had jerked his attention back to her and was now staring. "For my own protection, you see."

"You want to *box*." He opened and shut his mouth after he said it, as if he couldn't fully process what they were discussing. It seemed this conversation was going to be as humiliating as hers with her brother had been.

"You needn't bother telling me I'm too boring or plain or uninteresting to learn. Finn already told me that. And that the kind of woman who does do such a thing isn't anything like me. I can see you think me as foolish as he did." She pivoted to flee so she wouldn't have to see his pity. "I'll leave you to go find him and laugh at me together."

Before she could go, he caught her arm and turned her back gently. Immediately he released her and raised his hand to his chest almost like he'd been burned by the action. He cleared his throat. "No, I would say none of that. I'm taken aback, I admit, but I actually think ladies *should* know some basics when it comes to boxing. Men cannot be trusted on the whole and a well-placed punch can mean the difference between a fright and a horror."

"That's what *I* tried to say to him," she said.

"But he denied you," Sebastian said with a shake of his head.

She nodded. "He did. Strenuously."

"He's protective."

It wasn't a question, but a statement. Of course, Sebastian would know. She sighed. "I have no idea why. He thinks me dull and predictable, without enough spark to actually get myself in trouble."

Sebastian stared at her a beat, then two, long enough that she felt heat flood her cheeks. Then he said, "I could teach you."

Her lips parted in shock and she stared at him. "I'm sorry, what did you say?"

"I have a small practice ring in my home. If you came, I could show you some basics. For your own good."

She moved closer to him and could hardly contain her wonder and excitement. Once again this man offered to ride to her rescue, guiding her through her list without even knowing he was doing so. "You would do that? Even though my brother obviously disapproves."

That made him flinch and for a moment his gaze darted away. Then it returned and there was a hint of the heat she'd seen in him the previous week in her parlor. The heat she'd told herself she imagined and yet was there.

"He doesn't have to know, does he?" he asked.

There was something so wicked about that question. But she found herself nodding regardless. "Very well. When should I come?"

"Tomorrow afternoon?" he suggestion. "One o'clock if you can escape all chaperones."

"Easily," she said. "Boring and predictable, remember?"

"Not recently," he muttered, and then he bowed to her slightly. "I look forward to it. Now I should go mingle and try to avoid Lady Arabella and her mother as they set snares for the eligible gentlemen."

"Thank you," she said softly as he walked away, watching until he disappeared entirely into the little groups gathered around talking and sizing each other up.

There was a flutter in her chest as she made her way to the wall where she could have a moment's peace. It was excitement that she would yet again be able to cross something off her list. And nervousness that it would be Sebastian who helped her do so. But it was right, wasn't it? After all, aside from her own brother, he was the man she knew she could trust most in her life. The one who had no ulterior motives when it came to her.

Even if, in her deepest, hidden heart, she sometimes wished he did.

CHAPTER 6

Sebastian was nervous as he paced around his study, watching the clock on his mantel every time he pivoted. It was ridiculous. He didn't get *nervous*. He'd trained that sort of weakness out of himself. And even when he'd allowed himself that feeling in the past, it had never been about a woman. A friend, no less! Not even someone he was pursuing.

And yet, knowing Marianne would soon arrive to his home and they'd be alone again, he still felt this odd, fluttery discomfort in his chest.

"Why?" he grumbled out loud.

He had no answer for that. Nor for why he'd been thinking about Marianne so much in the last few weeks. Looking for her at gatherings, tracking her as she stood along walls or moved through crowds.

"It's only because you know Delacourt would be angry if he knew you were helping her with these odd requests," he finally said out loud.

That had to be true. He valued Delacourt's friendship above all others—they were almost like brothers. The worry about his friend's reaction could be the only thing making Marianne come to his mind so often. Nothing else.

"My lord?"

Sebastian jumped, for he hadn't heard his butler knock. He pivoted to face the older man. "Yes, Jenkins?"

"Lady Marianne is here," he said. "I've shown her to the parlor, as you requested, and told her you would join her shortly."

"Very good, thank you," Sebastian said. When his servant had excused himself, he turned to the mirror above the mantel, straightening and fixing himself before he headed down the hallway toward the parlor. His heart was beating hard in his chest. He scowled as if that would fix it, but of course it didn't.

Nor did it get better when he opened the parlor door and found Marianne standing at the fireplace, examining the line of miniatures arranged along the mantelpiece, a small smile on her face. When she turned to look at him, he saw her. Saw her like it was the first time.

She had a softly rounded face with fetching pink in the apples of her cheeks. Her brown eyes didn't yank a man in from across a room, but they were bright and kind. Her lips were full and a rosy color. And she had such delicate hands, which were currently fluttering at her sides as she drew a sharp breath.

"Sebastian?" she said. "Are you well?"

He jerked from the odd spell that had been woven over him and stepped forward, hand extended to her. "Of course," he said. "Welcome, my lady. It's a pleasure to see you, I'm glad you could escape."

She smiled as she squeezed his hand gently with both of hers, the warmth of her seeping through his gloves. "I wouldn't have missed it. I was terrified all morning that you would change your mind and send word for me not to come after all."

He wrinkled his brow. "And why would I do that?"

The flush of her cheeks darkened even more and her gaze flitted away from him. He oddly wanted to bring it back, make her hold his stare indefinitely as she cupped his fingers in her hands. "I'm sure you have far better things to do than to spend time with me."

He blinked at the statement. In this moment he could think of nothing he'd rather do than exactly that. Not one singular thing.

He cleared his throat. "You're my friend, Marianne. Any time I spend with you is more than worth the time, I assure you."

Her smile grew a fraction. "Thank you."

He pulled from her grip at last. "Er…yes…well, let's begin, shall we?"

He strode to the parlor door and she followed, falling into pace beside him as they moved down the long hallway toward one of the many other parlors that he had long ago outfitted as a practice space for fencing and boxing.

When he opened the door and motioned her in she did so, He followed her into the room while he tugged his gloves off and pushed them into his pocket. He heard her catch of breath as she looked around. He'd had many mirrors installed around the walls of the room so he could see his form when he worked on either sport and bright light sparkled in from the large windows across the room that looked out over his vast garden. A small boxing ring was roped off in the center of the room.

"Oh!" she gasped. "Is this what these sorts of places look like in the clubs?"

He shrugged. "The rings are bigger and there is more than one in the room, so more men can practice. But yes. It's something like this."

She pivoted toward him and delight brightened her face as she clasped her hands together. He found he liked delighting her.

"It really is something," she breathed. "Though I cannot picture fully what happens here."

"Then allow me to show you," he said, and moved toward her. He took her hand and turned it over in his own, noting how her short gloves fastened at her wrist. "Now, if we're going to do this properly, we would be wearing far fewer clothes."

Her mouth dropped open slightly. "Oh?" she croaked out and her nervousness was plain.

He smiled as he lifted her gaze to his. "But perhaps we'll just do this…"

And then he slipped a finger beneath her glove and gently unfastened the button.

Marianne could hardly breathe as she stared at her hand, watching as Sebastian slipped the little pearl button away from the loop of thread which held it in place. He seemed to move shockingly slow as he tugged each finger away and then removed the glove. At some point he had done the same with his own and his rough fingers glided across her skin as he did so.

She lifted her gaze to his and found him watching her closely as he did the same with her opposite glove. He folded them both and placed them into the pocket of his jacket. She swallowed because there seemed to be something so intimate about him taking a piece of her clothing and tucking it away into his pocket like it meant something. Even more intimate was that it was a piece of her clothing that he, himself, had removed.

"Don't be afraid," he said softly.

She shook her head. "I'm not afraid," she whispered in return, but it was a lie. In this moment, she felt afraid, but she didn't know why. It wasn't about the boxing, that was for certain, for she knew Sebastian would never harm her.

"You're trembling," he said.

"Not because I'm afraid," she said without thinking.

His pupils dilated and at last he turned away from her. He cleared his throat. "It's good you're wearing a short-sleeved gown—it will give you more mobility."

As he spoke he removed his jacket and carefully folded it over the back of a nearby chair. He unfastened his cufflinks and placed them there as well, and then began to roll up his sleeves.

She stared at he did so, revealing finely defined forearms lightly peppered with dark blonde hair. Good Lord, had she ever seen a man's forearm before? Were they all so…so attractive? She wanted to reach out and trace the skin there, feel if he was soft or hard, discover the shape of him.

"Hold your hands like this," he said, and lifted his fists so they partially blocked his face.

She tried to focus on what he was saying and doing and lifted her hands to copy him as best she could. "Like this?"

He stepped forward and adjusted her gently, lifting one hand, setting the other at a different angle. Then he touched her clenched fist, cupping it with his big hand.

"Your only problem is that you shouldn't trap your thumbs. Here, remove them."

"Why?" she asked as she tried to keep her breath while he helped her.

"Because if you threw a hard enough punch, you could break the bone and you definitely don't want to do that."

She winced at the thought. "My brother said boxing was violent."

"It's a combat sport," Sebastian said with a small smile. "So yes, it's violent. But in the best matches there is great respect. A desire to compete well with a good opponent. Friendships can be made in the ring more often than broken."

"Men are so odd," Marianne said with a sigh.

"Are we?" Sebastian laughed. "How so?"

"If *I* were to punch another lady, I doubt we would be friends," Marianne said.

He tilted his head back and laughed, the sound working through her body in unexpected ways. Ways that made her tingle. "I suppose not. I'm having a hard time picturing you throwing a punch at some lady's head."

"I hope not, as that is what you're to teach me to do."

He lifted his brows. "Oh, is that your true purpose, my dear? To rampage through Society, knocking out beauties left and right?"

She smiled, but there was a faint sting in her chest. "Can you imagine? I would be well and fully shunned then. They'd have every excuse to stop inviting me to their soirees."

"You think they don't want you there?"

"I'm a reminder that failure is a possibility for every lady," she said, and saw the flicker of pity in his stare. She recoiled from it. "Honestly, this cannot be an interesting topic to you, Sebastian. Won't you show me what to do next?"

He hesitated for a moment, as if he wanted to say something else to her, but then he nodded. "Of course."

For the next half an hour he showed her various punches, letting her practice the moves of them over and over in the air. Though she felt awkward at first, as she had always been taught not to move her body too broadly, never to take up too much space, as she became accustomed to doing so she found it...liberating.

He smiled after a while. "Why don't we take a break? Rest your arms before the next part in the lesson."

She shook out her tingling limbs. "That's likely a good idea."

He motioned to a sideboard along the back wall of the room and she flushed as she realized a tea set was waiting there. She'd been so wrapped up, she hadn't realized anyone had come in with it. He poured her a cup and she drank it greedily.

"This sort of exertion really parches a person," she said, watching him over the lip of the cup.

"Indeed it does," he murmured but didn't meet her eyes.

She cleared her throat. "I wanted to...ask you something."

He did look at her then. "About what you've learned?"

She shifted with discomfort. "Not exactly. You said something earlier and I-I shouldn't question you about it, but I find I must."

"That sounds dire." Sebastian held out a hand toward two chairs before the window, faced out to look at the view. She took one and focused on the green expanse outside rather than her companion. She didn't want to see his pity again.

"When I arrived, you told me you were my friend," she said. "But that…that isn't true, is it?"

"You don't think of me as a friend?" he asked, and there was hesitation in his tone.

She caught her breath. "Well, no. I mean, yes, I see you as my friend. I have few enough of those, so I cherish them. I meant more that I…I cannot be *your* friend, can I?"

He was silent a long moment, just watching her through a hooded gaze that left his emotions unreadable. "You think me incapable?"

"No, not at all. I only mean that *Finn* is your friend. Your best friend. I'm just the annoying little sister who you are forced to be kind to. Aren't I?"

She wished she weren't asking the question. Said out loud, it made her feel so needy and pathetic. But she wanted things to be clear between them, perhaps because the last few times they'd spent together had felt so confused.

He leaned forward in his chair, and though there was a reasonable distance between them it still felt suddenly close in the large room. His bright blue eyes bore into hers, holding her steady and keeping her from turning away. "When we were all children, I suppose I once thought of you as the tagalong sibling who interrupted our fun and forced Finn to run after you, making certain you were unharmed."

She smiled, for she hadn't heard Sebastian call her brother by his first name in years.

"*But*," he said, stressing the word gently, "that feeling faded swiftly enough. Soon I looked forward to seeing you as much as I did him. And as we've become adults, I promise you that I value your friendship as entirely separate from his."

There was a charged moment that hung between them and then he sat back, all casual confidence again. "If you don't believe me, please take the fact that I would court his wrath by inviting you into my lair and teaching you to throw a punch against his wishes."

She smothered a smile and looked around. "It isn't much of a lair, Sebastian."

He caught his breath. "Slander! I'll have you know I've worked hard to make it so."

"Please, you have pretty parlors and a lovely dining room. This room here is unusual in its purpose, but there's light and happiness in the layout. It all verifies what I've long suspected."

"And what is that?"

"You're not the rake you pretend to be," she said.

If she thought he would smile, he didn't. Instead, he moved forward again and this time his eyes smoldered when he held hers. "I promise you, my dear, I very much am."

She swallowed, uncertain what to say to him, but he didn't seem to require a response because he pushed to his feet and strode away from her back toward the middle of the room. "Let's continue, shall we?"

She pursed her lips as she followed him and watched as he positioned himself back where they had started. She looked toward the ring behind him. "Do you not use that?"

He glanced over his shoulder. "Well, yes, of course. During sparring and if I host a real match."

"But we're not going to use it?"

He smiled. "I wasn't certain you'd want to climb over the ropes in your dress. Or be trapped in the ring with me."

She returned his smile. "I've climbed over plenty of fences in the country. I don't see how this would be much different. And perhaps I've learned so much from you in the last hour that *you'll* feel trapped in the ring with me."

His grin widened as he stepped toward the ring and pressed a foot to the lower rope and a hand to the higher one to open a bigger space for her. "I accept that challenge, my lady. Please, after you."

There was a flutter in her chest as she moved toward the slightly raised ring. She'd teased, something entirely against her character and yet always felt natural with Sebastian, but now she stared at the gap between the ropes and was uncertain how to proceed without dropping herself head over heels into the ring.

He held out a hand. "Or are you having second thoughts?"

"No," she muttered, and took the hand he offered. He gripped her firmly, steadying her as she stepped onto the narrow ledge of the elevated platform. "Do you have any suggestions?"

"I think if you just lift your skirt a little higher, you'll find it easier."

She glanced up at him. A lady didn't show a gentleman her ankles or calves. He would see both if she did as he suggested. "Will you close your eyes?"

He shook his head with a chuckle. "You think I haven't seen such things before."

"Not such things on me," she said with a playful glare for him.

He obliged her by shutting his eyes. "Go ahead."

She lifted her skirts, leaned on his hand and ducked under the top rope to slip into the ring. When she released his hand and smoothed her dress down, she said, "You may look now."

"I feel as though I've missed out," he said, ducking under the rope himself with effortless grace. "Perhaps next time."

"You're a cad," she said.

"Proudly so." He broadened his stance and lifted his hands up. "Now, show me if you recall what you've leaned today and punch my palms."

She lifted her brows. "You want me to punch you?"

"No, most definitely not. I'll hold my hands up, you try to hit them square in my palm."

She shifted with discomfort. She'd never struck another person in her life, palms or not. But Sebastian seemed certain, so she moved into the stance he had taught her earlier in the lesson and took a deep breath.

"Perfect," he said softly. "You are perfect."

She blinked at that statement. He meant her form, she supposed, but the compliment still hit her in a deeper way. She pushed her giddy, foolish reaction aside and swung, connecting with his palm with solid *thwack*.

"Very good, Marianne!" he crowed, sounding as excited as she felt. "Steady yourself a little more. Pivot your hips as you turn, that is what puts the power in your punch."

She adjusted herself and swung again, hitting him in the center of the palm again with a louder reverberation. He was grinning fully now, his blue eyes dancing. "Again!"

She did, over and over, each time gaining more confidence. Finally, she put all her body weight into the throw, hit his palm and her feet tangled, sending her forward with the momentum.

He caught her under her arms as she collided with his broad chest and tugged her a little closer to keep her from falling or knocking him down. It felt like everything in the room, even her heartbeat, came to a sudden stop as she stared up into his face, which was now mere inches from her own. To her surprise, he was looking down at her with the same intense focus. His gaze slipped to her mouth and a riot of sensation rushed through her body at that motion.

Sensation that only increased when he began to lower his mouth toward hers. Was he going to kiss her? Right here in the middle of the big parlor, with sunlight streaming across them like a spotlight, with his arms around her and her chest flush to his? She found her eyes fluttering shut in anticipation as she lifted her lips.

But he didn't kiss her. It felt like forever passed and then he gently set her back on her feet and steadied her as she opened her eyes, heat flaring her cheeks.

"You…it's easy to get excited," he said, his voice a little shaky. "And lose your balance. So you set your feet each time, careful of your environment so you don't make a…make a mistake."

She stepped back, hoping her humiliation wasn't clear on her face. God, he had to have known she thought he'd kiss her. She hadn't been subtle about it, offering herself to him like some silly wanton.

But of course that hadn't been his intent. She wasn't the kind of woman he wanted. She was just…Marianne.

"Yes, I see," she said. "You know, this has been wonderful. I've enjoyed it far more than I thought possible. But it's getting late in the afternoon and I must return home. I'm certain you have better things to do, as well."

"Yes, of course," he said, and moved to the ropes where he pushed them wide and offered his hand once more for assistance, though he turned his head away. This time when she took it, she shivered, for his touch meant more after what had just occurred between them.

Or not occurred. Nothing had occurred after all. Just her foolish imaginings.

She smoothed herself back into place as she reached the ground and forced herself not to watch him come out of the ring after her.

"Let me take you to the foyer and ask for your carriage to be brought around," he said, motioning to the door. She followed him, this time not walking beside him as they made their way back down the twisting halls to where she had begun her day. He gave his instructions to the servant there and together they stood, suddenly awkward as they waited for her vehicle to come up from the stable. She searched for something to say that would return their banter to normalcy, return their friendship so he'd know she wasn't upset or going to do or say something foolish.

"Are you…are you going to the Brighthollow ball next week?" she asked.

He blinked. "Er, I suppose so. I think I recall an invitation from the duke and duchess in the pile yesterday. I assume that means you will be in attendance, as well?"

"Yes. My aunt will wish it. She is obsessed with this new batch of ducal marriages that have flooded Society in the last year or two.

All true love, it seems." She shifted and wished she hadn't said the last. "At any rate, I suppose I'll see you there then."

The carriage mercifully came and she clamored up as soon as the step was lowered, without waiting for assistance from either Sebastian or any of the servants. Sebastian stepped forward and closed the door himself. The window was open and he leaned in slightly.

"I look forward to it, Marianne. I hope you'll save a dance for me."

She nodded and he stepped away, tapping on the carriage side so that her driver would go. But as soon as she exited his drive, she sank down a little lower in her seat. She should have been more than satisfied with what she'd done today. She'd crossed off another item on Claudia's list and in the end Sebastian had returned to his normal self, at least in word.

But there was something that felt so off about everything between them now. Something had shifted when she'd believed he was going to kiss her, but he hadn't. She feared what that would mean.

She looked down at her hands clenched in her lap and realized for the first time that she was still not wearing her gloves. Sebastian had removed them. He'd put them in his pocket.

And he still had them. She shivered at the recognition of such an intimate thing. And then tried to push away all the meaning she wanted to ascribe to it, to the afternoon and to the intimacy of his holding her.

She was traveling down a dangerous road by wanting to see more in his bright blue eyes than playful flirtation. And if she wanted to remain his friend, she would have to control herself better in the future.

CHAPTER 7

One of Sebastian's favorite places in London was the Donville Masquerade, a notorious underground hell that provided to its members the unabashed freedom to explore sin. He came here to play, to forget, to bury himself in pleasure when pain came to visit.

But tonight, standing at the bar with Delacourt, he didn't feel his usual sense of calm and excitement as he looked across the writhing, sensual crowd.

No, he felt the opposite. He felt...wrong.

"Are you brooding to attract the attention of the ladies, or is something truly on your mind?" Delacourt drawled as he sipped a drink. It was his third of the night and his friend's voice was slow with the edges of drunkenness.

Sebastian drew a long breath as he looked at Delacourt. They'd met here for a night of careless fun, but he felt awkward around his best friend now. Guilty, even though he hadn't really done anything wrong.

Only that wasn't true. Three days ago, he'd gone against what he knew were Delacourt's wishes and spent an afternoon with Marianne in his boxing ring. He'd teased her and taught her and felt more than he should about the exercise. Not to mention, he'd kept the gloves she'd left behind that day, even though he could have sent them back to her once he realized they were still in his pocket.

Worse, in that moment when she'd stumbled against him and everything had become close and hot and slow, he'd wanted to kiss her.

Actually, that wasn't the right word for it. He *hadn't* wanted to kiss her. A kiss could be chaste and sweet and romantic. What he'd wanted to do was dig his fingers into her dark hair and tilt her mouth up farther and devour her. He'd wanted to cup her backside and grind her into him until there was no doubt what he wanted. He'd wanted to push her down onto the floor of that boxing ring and lick her until she convulsed in pleasure. He'd wanted to roll her over and flip up her skirts and fuck her so that she truly understood the word he'd taught her over a week before.

"Ramsbury. *Sebastian!*"

He blinked to clear those erotic, unexpected, *unwanted* thoughts from his mind and refocused on Delacourt, who was now staring at him with true concern.

"My apologies," he said. "Woolgathering, I suppose."

"About what?"

He almost laughed. Delacourt would have an apoplexy if he knew the answer to that question. After he'd punched Sebastian to a bloody pulp that was. "Nothing of consequence," Sebastian lied. "How is your sister?"

"Marianne?" Delacourt asked, his brow wrinkling at what he must have seen as a change of subject even though it was decidedly not. "She's fine, I suppose. Still mourning her old friend, I think, but otherwise well."

Sebastian frowned. "Yes…Lady Claudia."

"Broadsmoore's sister, though he seems to mourn her little enough. Marianne has been friends with her since her disaster of a coming out all those years ago."

"Yes," Sebastian said softly, and tried to picture Lady Claudia. He was ashamed to find he couldn't, despite the fact that she was so important to Marianne.

"Spinsters of a feather, Marianne always said," Delacourt continued. "I had always hoped that my sister might have a chance at a marriage in the future, someone to protect her better than I can. But she seems resigned to her life as it is now."

Sebastian wrinkled his brow. He might have said the same about Marianne if pressed a few weeks ago, but her recent actions made him question that statement now. He realized all her odd behavior had come since her friend's untimely death. Did that mean Marianne actually *did* want more and Delacourt hadn't seen it? Or was it merely grief driving her...well, some might call at least a few of them reckless actions?

"Why the question about Marianne?" Delacourt asked, his gaze narrowing and becoming harder.

"She's my friend, just as you have been, so I'm always curious about her welfare," Sebastian said with a dismissive shrug even though that explanation felt sour on his tongue. Wrong.

"Hmmm," Delacourt said as he looked out into the crowd. "Just don't take advantage. It's the one thing I've ever asked of you."

"Yes, I know," Sebastian said. "I assure you I'd never go too far."

Except even as he said those words, he saw Marianne's face again, turned up toward his, her dark eyes fluttering shut on a sigh as she waited for him to do the impossible and take her lips.

"Excellent. But I don't wish to talk about her anymore, not here," Delacourt said. "We came here to get our cocks wet. I intend to do so and I suggest you do the same." He patted Sebastian's arm before he eased into the writhing crowd and into the waiting arms of a comely woman in a mask who had been watching them from a table for the last ten minutes.

Sebastian saw plenty of women who would offer the same solace to him. Normally he wouldn't think twice to take it. To drown himself in a warm, wet body that clenched his with pleasure.

Only tonight, as he stood at that bar, he found he didn't...he didn't want to do that. He didn't want some anonymous woman in a pretty mask to put her hands and mouth on him. What he wanted, he feared was destined to destroy him.

So he stayed right where he was, nursing a drink, and trying not to think of brown eyes and soft skin and a smile that seemed to light up the world when he coaxed it. He tried not to think of Marianne.

Marianne stood before her wardrobe, staring at the row of gowns hanging there as she and her maid tried to decide on which one she would wear to the Brighthollow ball in a few days' time. They were all beautiful, of course. Finn had always provided her with a generous allowance for her clothing and she had allowed herself the pleasure of pretty fabrics over the years.

But none of them were *daring*. Claudia's list said, *Wear Something Daring.*

"I've always thought the blue was pretty," her maid, Hannah, suggested hesitantly.

Marianne blinked. She must have been staring forever if Hannah had that tone to her voice. It was a mix between concern and mild annoyance.

She sighed. "What do you think a daring gown would be like?"

Hannah turned toward her slightly. "My lady?"

Heat was beginning to flood Marianne's cheeks, so she refused to look at her servant and forced herself to continue. "It's just that all of these are rather…boring, aren't they? What would a lady wear if she wished to be *daring*? Would it merely be a bold color? Is it a cut to the gown? Or is it something in her character? A confidence?"

She hoped it wasn't the last, for she couldn't alter herself like she would a gown.

Hannah shifted. "I suppose it's all of those things. Why do you ask, my lady?"

"I don't know." Marianne paced away and stood at her window looking down at the dark garden below. "I'm just wondering if I could use a little more *daring* in my life."

Hannah was quiet a moment and when Marianne dared to look at her, she was back to staring at the gowns. She fingered the frilly puffed sleeve of one of them. It was cut from a bold pink that had then been covered with lace and ribbon.

"This is a pretty color," Hannah said. "It draws the eye, which I suppose is part of being considered daring."

Marianne took a step closer. "I see."

"I suppose it might be daring to—" Hannah hesitated again and looked at her. "Well, we could remove this lace overlay here."

She motioned to the bodice of the dress and Marianne's eyes widened. "That would...that would reveal a great deal more bosom."

"Not a wrong amount, though. Just enough. I'd also remove some of these frills, let more shoulder peek out at the edge here, you see?"

Marianne came closer as Hannah folded in some of the details. She tried to picture herself in a gown that exposed so much. It was terrifying. But then, wasn't that what Claudia's list was all about? Living life, despite the fear?

"What else?" Marianne croaked.

Hannah seemed much more invested now that her suggestions hadn't been roundly rejected. "When I fix your hair for gatherings, I often do it somewhat plainly. I could fix it differently. Perhaps we could even put some jewels or other decoration woven into the locks."

"Oh," Marianne said, her mind going to her disastrous coming out. "But they'll look at me."

Hannah's gaze shifted to her and gentled. "I believe that is what daring requires, my lady."

"I suppose so."

"Are you well?" Hannah asked.

"I'm not exactly sure," Marianne murmured, then smiled at her servant to reassure her. "Let's make the adjustments to the pink gown if it can be managed before the Brighthollow ball. I would like to try daring at least once in my life."

There was a surprising burst of excitement in Hannah's eyes at that statement. "Yes! Yes, my lady. I'll be sure the gown is ready by the ball. Is there anything else?"

"No, I'll ring when I'm ready to retire," Marianne said, and watched as Hannah took the pink gown and left the room.

Once she was gone, Marianne returned to the window and the garden below. It seemed she would have her daring gown, a technical check off Claudia's list. But could she manage the rest of the costume? Could she find the confidence within herself to bear the potential stares that might follow such a change?

And with Sebastian there, could she bear it if he didn't notice the change at all? Both seemed equally awful results.

"I suppose we'll see," she mused before she took a place before her fire, swept up the book she'd been trying to read for days, and tried to concentrate. But her mind kept shifting to all the possibilities of what could happen when she walked into the ball and showed the world a face she'd never even thought she possessed.

CHAPTER 8

Marianne stared at herself in the full-length mirror in her dressing room and shook her head for what felt like the tenth time in as many minutes. She hardly recognized herself.

"You did wonders in such a short time, Hannah, I truly appreciate it," she whispered because she felt her servant staring and didn't want her to think the silence was due to disappointment.

No, that wasn't the emotion in her chest at all.

"Thank you. You really do look lovely, Lady Marianne."

"I assume my brother has arrived to escort Aunt Beulah and me to the ball. Do you think you could go down to them and tell them I'll only be a moment more?"

Hannah's brow wrinkled a fraction and then she nodded. "Of course, my lady."

She scurried from the room and Marianne looked at herself again. Where she normally had a plain bun at her nape, Hannah had wrapped and curled and braided her dark locks until they shone and fluttered in a more fetching way. She'd also put some jeweled clips into her hair, ones once worn by her late mother. They did draw the eye.

She'd lightly rouged Marianne's cheeks and lips, just enough to give color. A good thing, since she knew she was more pale than usual thanks to her nerves about the night.

And then there was the dress. She'd spun herself into knots trying to picture what it would look like. She'd feared looking almost naked with all the frills removed. And yet that was not the effect. Oh yes, there was more shoulder revealed, more of the curve of her bosom. But the increased simplicity of the gown actually made her feel...pretty.

She hadn't felt pretty in a very long time.

She shook her head and turned away from the mirror before she took her reticule, complete with her dance card for the evening, and made her way downstairs where her family waited for her. She drew a deep breath and smoothed her skirt before she entered the parlor.

Her aunt and brother were standing by the sideboard and he was smiling as she finished a drink. They both turned when she entered the room and she saw their expressions change to ones of twin shock.

"I-I'm sorry I was late," she stammered, knowing her cheeks were turning the same color as her dress beneath their intense scrutiny.

"Marianne!" Aunt Beulah gasped. "You look..."

She trailed off and Marianne found herself smoothing her skirt again. "It's too much?"

"No," Finn said, stepping forward. "You look lovely, Mari."

"Very lovely, my dear," Beulah reassured her.

They both seemed sincere enough and Marianne relaxed a fraction. That was the first test passed. Neither of them had called her a jezebel or laughed at her for trying to be bolder.

"Would you like a drink?" her brother asked.

"Oh, no, I couldn't," she said. "And I've delayed us long enough. We should depart, should we not?"

He stared at her a moment and then slightly inclined his head. "Certainly."

He took their aunt's arm and together they went out to where the carriage awaited them. Marianne tensed as he helped her in beside Beulah. She could feel Finn watching her, reading her. He had questions, it seemed, even if he had no judgments. And she didn't want to answer those questions. She didn't want to hear all his protection come to the forefront. She didn't want to feel him watching her all night as he tried to keep her from any harm or from any change that would help her be, even momentarily, something more than a boring spinster.

But somehow he didn't ask during the short ride. Beulah kept him busy discussing a play Finn had apparently seen a few nights before, and that allowed Marianne the ability to look out the window, take a few breaths and try to ready her mind for what was about to happen.

They came into the line of carriages that wrapped around the circular drive at the beautiful home of the Duke and Duchess of Brighthollow. She didn't know either of them well, though she did know the duke's sister, Elizabeth. The young lady hadn't been a wallflower or a spinster, per se, but it had been clear she'd never enjoyed Society much. Marianne had always liked her.

Finn helped them each down and once again escorted their aunt up into the house and the line of those greeting the duke and duchess. Since they were later than most, it all moved along swiftly and she found herself greeting the handsome duke and the truly beautiful duchess. The woman seemed to shine, with her bright blue eyes and sleek black hair. Marianne felt dowdy, not daring, next to her, dress or no dress.

And yet Her Grace caught both of Marianne's hands and squeezed after they were introduced. "Oh, Lady Marianne, I've heard so much about you from our dear Lizzie."

Marianne blushed at being remembered. "How lovely. I was just thinking of her as we came up the stairs. Is she in London?"

"No, you may have heard of her recent marriage," the duchess said with a quick glance and smile toward the duke. "She is honey-mooning right now at our country estate."

"Ah, yes, I'd heard of her marriage." Marianne tried to maintain her smile. She hadn't been jealous of Elizabeth when the news had spread. There was no one in the world who deserved more happiness than the kind, quiet young woman. But she certainly had felt a little deflated by it. She sometimes allowed herself to believe that after a certain point, one just gave up on the idea of a union.

Any time that was thwarted it made her feel like a failure.

"But we're hoping to coax the couple to Town sometime after the summer," the duke said, taking his wife's hand and sliding into the crook of his arm with an indulgent look at her. "If we do, we'll be certain to hold a soiree and invite you all. I know she'd love to see you."

"That would be wonderful, thank you," Marianne said, and then nodded to excuse herself as another group of stragglers entered the foyer and the duke and duchess turned to greet them.

She followed Finn and Aunt Beulah into the ballroom. They were announced and the eyes of the room turned toward them. Normally that didn't trouble her, for the people around them were always looking through her, looking at Phineas. He was a catch, after all.

But tonight their gazes lingered on her. Whispers began as ladies talked behind their fans and gentlemen who she was certain didn't even realize she existed now took a longer look at her in her new gown.

It seemed daring was, indeed, a draw. It made her a little hot and dizzy, frankly. Were they speaking unkindly of her? Did they think her a fool for putting herself on display as she had?

Their aunt excused herself and made her way toward her group of friends, and that left Marianne alone with Finn. He turned toward her, her brow slightly wrinkled.

"Marianne," he said, and in his voice she heard all those questions she'd wanted to avoid in the carriage.

But before he could ask them, a voice from one of the nearby groups called out, "Delacourt!"

He looked toward them with a flash of annoyance and then back toward her. "Forgive me. I have something to discuss with those gentlemen. I hope you'll save me a dance later."

Marianne almost laughed. Her dance card was only ever filled by Finn's name or the occasional name of a gentleman who was his friend, like Sebastian. The idea she had to *save* anything was absurd.

But she was happy enough for the freedom from whatever questions he would ask and waved him to go before she started through the crowd herself on her way to the wall.

"Good evening, Lady Marianne," a gentleman said as she passed him, and she inclined her head as she continued her way through the crowd. Had that been Mr. Lanford? The third son of Viscount Lanford? He hadn't spoken to her in years.

"Lady Marianne," came another voice of greeting, from another gentleman who nodded as she went by.

Yet another inclined his head with a brief smile. She was utterly confused as she reached the wall and took her normal place there to stare out at the crowd. Only this time some of them were looking back at her. It was entirely odd.

Normally it was only Sebastian who ever found her on the wall. And just as that thought entered her mind, she found him in the crowd. And he was, indeed, watching her as he often did. But tonight there was a different expression on his face than normal. It was more intense, more focused. She smiled at him and she saw him draw a breath in response.

He took a step her way and her heart leapt but before he could close the distance between them a gentleman stepped into her line of sight, closing her off from her view of Sebastian.

"Good evening, Lady Marianne," the man said.

She blinked. It was Mr. Lanford again, the first man who had greeted her as she made her way through the crowd a few moments before. "Mr. Lanford," she said, forcing her words out past a suddenly dry throat. "How nice to see you."

"And you," he said. "Since you have only just arrived, I hoped that your dance card might not be full yet and that you might honor me with the next."

He smiled as she said it and in her shock at the question she examined him. He didn't look to be making fun of her or be forced by some unknown reason to ask her for the dance. He seemed sincere, even if she didn't think she'd ever danced with him before.

She glanced over his shoulder, but found Sebastian was no longer where he'd been standing earlier. It seemed there would be no battle for her attention. She'd probably only imagined Sebastian's interest anyway. Once he realized he wouldn't be forced to entertain her, he'd likely been pleased and moved on to more interesting quarry.

"Lady Marianne?" Lanford said, a little more gently.

She forced a laugh. "Of course. I'd be happy to dance, with you, sir."

He held out an arm, which she took and then allowed him to lead her to the dancefloor and the quadrille that was just beginning.

Sebastian stood in a corner of the ballroom, drink clutched in his white-knuckled hand, and he watched Marianne. He had been doing the same all night, it seemed he couldn't stop himself, and so he'd seen her dancing virtually every dance. When she hadn't been spinning around the floor, she'd been chatting with gentlemen of varying quality. She'd also been watched by a great many others.

What was most interesting was how utterly unaware she seemed to be of the splash she was making just by wearing a more audacious gown and arranging her hair like a goddess who had deigned to come down from Mount Olympus and allow her subjects to worship.

She seemed equally unaware of how being an observer of it all made Sebastian burn. How *could* she be aware? Aside from one brief look at him after her arrival, she hadn't noticed him at all.

And now she smiled at the gentleman who was just leaving her side and noticed the next one who was stalking up on her, ready to stake his brief claim on her attention. But to Sebastian's surprise, she didn't look excited by the next attendee, but exhausted. She ducked to the left, obviously pretending she didn't see him and then weaved her way through the crowd.

Where was she going?

The terrace. She was escaping to the terrace. He realized he was moving before he meant to do it. Following her. Why, he didn't want to examine. After all, he couldn't begrudge her this attention. Couldn't begrudge her looking beautiful and having others notice it. Delacourt had said it at the Donville Masquerade a few days before that he'd hoped Marianne might have still had a chance at something beyond the life of a spinster.

And yet Sebastian still found himself opening the terrace door he'd watched her go through moments before and stepping out into the cool night air to look for her.

She was standing at the terrace wall, staring out into the inky night. There were a few lanterns lit for those who might come out and in the dim light of the one she stood near, he saw her discomfort. Her overwhelm. And once again he was mobbed by questions about her recent behavior.

He stepped toward her and she turned to face him with a jump of surprise.

"Marianne," he said, without preamble. "Why are you doing all this?"

She shook her head and lifted a hand to her chest, forcing him to follow the action almost against his will. "Sebastian, you frightened me."

"Why?" he insisted.

Her brow wrinkled. "Doing...*what?* I came to a ball where I was invited and—"

He shook his head. "The drinking, the swearing, the fighting, that—" He swallowed as he looked up and down her body now that he was close enough to really enjoy it. "That dress. Why are you trying to be someone you're not?"

Her face fell at that question and the hurt was as evident as the fullness of her lips. "Someone I'm not," she repeated. He nodded slowly. She folded her arms, her expression hardening from hurt to anger. "Because I could never be so interesting, is that what you mean?"

He drew back at her tart tone and the flash of her eyes. "No. I'd never say that."

"No, it would be impolite to point out that I'm a dowdy spinster doing things she shouldn't be out of some pathetic attempt to be someone she isn't." She tilted her head. "Oh, wait, that's *exactly* what you just did."

He flinched. "That wasn't my intention. I worded it badly. Let me start again. Something is clearly wrong, Marianne. Or...different, anyway. Your friend died and suddenly you have started doing all these out of character things. I worry about you. As a *friend.*"

She shook her head. "Oh, please. No matter what you said to me before, no matter how you try to pretend otherwise, we both know that you are only my friend out of loyalty to my brother. And out of pity. Someone like you could never understand someone like me."

He moved closer, almost impossibly close now. He could smell the lemon and rose petal scent of her hair, see the shine of unshed tears in her dark eyes.

"I *know* what it's like to want to be someone different. Anyone but myself." He heard those words he never spoke out loud leave his lips and wished them back almost instantly.

She stared up at him, but her expression remained doubtful, hurt, angry. "Liar," she whispered, and then moved to step around him.

He caught her arm almost out of instinct and brought her back to him in one gentle tug. She fell against his chest just as she had in his boxing ring days before, and once again she stared up at him, her breath short, her pupils dilated, her fingers tense against his chest.

But tonight he had no ability to fight what he wanted. Tonight he cupped her cheek, splaying his fingers against impossible softness, bent his head and kissed her.

CHAPTER 9

Sebastian's mouth came down on hers and Marianne was immediately drowning. There was nothing cruel in the kiss, despite the heated, emotional exchange that had somehow led to it, but there was nothing gentle either. It was…claiming. His lips were firm and warm, and when she gasped in surprise, he traced the entrance to her mouth with his tongue.

It should have felt strange, wrong, but it didn't. It was like sinking into a warm bath after a long day or finally getting to have dessert after a boring supper party. Something she had been anticipating even if she'd thought otherwise and now it was here and it was everything.

She opened to him, she had no other choice, for she was being swept out to sea by an expert sailor. He tasted her, there was no other way to describe it and she shivered even though the way his tongue swirled around hers made her hot, not cold. He tilted his head, angling for more of her, like he wanted to devour her, like he needed her as much as he needed his next breath.

Certainly, she needed him. Her thoughts, her fears…they all faded away and she was left with only sensation. His heated mouth, his talented tongue, the way the fingers of one hand stroked her jawline so gently while the other hand shifted away from their grip on her arm and slid around her waist to hold her even more firmly against his chest. It seemed he knew she was being lost and he wanted to anchor her.

Her body shook, heat flowed from the place where they kissed, spread through her body like tendrils that touched every nerve, every limb, every place that could throb or tingle or tense with pleasure. She wanted more. She didn't care that they were on a terrace at a ball filled with people. She didn't care that her brother was only feet away. She didn't care that this was Sebastian, a man who flirted and teased but never meant anything he ever said.

She wanted everything. She wanted the things married ladies stopped talking about when women like her entered a room. She wanted scandal and heat and passion like it was her birthright.

It was as if Sebastian read her mind, because in that moment he pulled away. He continued to hold her, but his mouth parted from hers and he stared down at her in the dim light, their panting breaths matching.

He said nothing, his expression revealed nothing. At last, he stepped back, steadying her carefully before he removed his hands from her trembling body.

"Forgive me," he murmured, and then he pivoted and staggered to the door back into the ballroom, leaving her alone on the terrace once more.

She spun back around to look at the garden again, her hands shaking so hard that she had to press them into the uneven stone of the terrace wall to ground herself. Sebastian had kissed her. Kissed her like he was worshipping her, like he needed her.

That wasn't true, of course. The heat of the moment, the argument, had caused him to lose his senses. When those senses returned, of course he had walked away in regret. But he'd still kissed her. And now she would never not know what his lips tasted like, what his hands felt like clenching against her back as he tugged her what felt like impossibly close.

Would it change whatever was between them? The friendship she always doubted and yet depended on, almost as much as she had depended on Claudia? Tears filled her eyes at the thought. She'd already lost one of them.

"Lady Marianne?"

She drew a breath. It was a gentleman's voice at the door, but not Sebastian's. She turned and found Lord Beckington standing at the terrace door. He had a friendly smile and she forced herself to return the expression, if only so he wouldn't see her true, tangled feelings.

"Lord Beckington, good evening."

"I'm so glad to have found you," he said. "Do you have space left on your dance card, by chance?"

She swallowed. She'd come out here to avoid all that, but now the idea of distracting herself was tempting. "I…I do, my lord. The next, in fact."

He held out a hand and she moved toward him, back to the ball-room, back to reality. A reality that could never be the same again.

Sebastian fought for breath as sat in his carriage, gripping the edge of the seat as it rattled along the cobblestone streets toward his home. He had said goodbye to no one after leaving the terrace, but had gone straight for the escape of his carriage. He'd not found his hosts, not Delacourt, certainly not Marianne.

God's teeth, Marianne. What had he been thinking kissing her? On a terrace. At a ball. Where anyone could have seen them.

Actually, he knew what he'd been thinking. That only made it worse. He'd wanted her. The thwarted kiss at his home a week before had haunted him ever since, even when he tried to pretend it away. He'd wanted her and that want had become so loud in his mind that he couldn't deny it anymore.

Now he could taste her on his tongue, he could feel the way she'd trembled against his fingers, he could hear the soft sound of pleasure she'd made in her throat, one she probably didn't even realize she'd sighed into the dark, into him like a breath of life.

It all ricocheted through him and he pulsed with the power of his need for her. For *Marianne*. The last woman in the world he should want for so many reasons they could hardly be counted. The chief amongst them being that he'd been forbidden to pursue her by a man he cared about like a brother.

One didn't sport with a woman like Marianne. And since Sebastian was not interested in anything but sport, what he had done was...*wrong* wasn't a strong enough word. He despised himself for it. For his lack of control, for his lack of forethought. He could lose a friend for this. Two friends, for regardless of what she thought, he *did* view Marianne as that. In fact, sometimes he looked forward to seeing her even more than he did Delacourt.

Only one didn't go around kissing friends like that, did they? They didn't picture doing even more, like pushing her into the dark corner of the terrace and dropping to his knees to taste her far more intimately until she panted his name while she shook with release against his tongue.

"Fuck," he grunted, trying to push those thoughts from his head. They wouldn't go and he was happy the carriage was pulling into his drive.

He exited the vehicle as soon as it stopped, waving off the servants who came to greet him, his butler at the door. Nothing mattered now except the pulse of need that wouldn't be denied. He strode straight upstairs to his chamber, locked the door behind himself and unfastened the fall front of his trousers.

His cock was half-hard already. It hadn't been anything less since he took Marianne in his arms. It took one stroke to go to full hardness and he sank into the settee before the fire, slouching as he began to tug with purpose.

And his betrayer of a mind took him once more to Marianne. Back on that terrace, but in the dark corner like his fantasies in the carriage. Would she taste sweet when...no, not *when*. This wasn't going to happen. It had to stop.

Still, he had to believe her gorgeous smell would permeate his entire being. He would find it just as intoxicating, *more* intoxicating, if he lifted her skirts and rubbed his cheek against her bare thighs. Her fingers would go into his hair, clenching there like she'd clenched them against his chest the last two times he'd held her.

And he would devour her like some kind of wicked wolf in a fairytale. He would taste every inch of her quivering flesh until she convulsed against him and left his chin covered in the proof of her pleasure. Only then would he cup her against him and take her. Hard and fast against the wall of a house while he kissed her so that her moans wouldn't be heard by all the very proper people just through the window around the bend of the terrace.

He came with such sudden power that his back curved off the settee. His heart was pounding, his hands shaking as his body came down from the high of fantasy and pleasure.

When was the last time he'd been so lost? He couldn't recall it. Clearly, he needed to fuck someone just so that this madness would stop. He needed to go back to the Donville Masquerade or a brothel or a former mistress and just let himself have what he clearly couldn't control.

Only he didn't want that. Impossibly, the idea was actually repellent. And so he sat there on his settee, staring into the fire as his heart rate finally slowed to normal, and hated himself instead. Because he deserved that. And because he had no idea how to change it now that the wheels of this runaway desire had been set fully into motion.

~

Marianne sat in her night-rail at the small table by her window, a candle burning low beside her and casting a small circle of light onto the list Claudia had left her. It was far too late at night to be doing this, but after the ball earlier, she hadn't been able to stop her busy mind and there was no way sleep could possibly come now.

She stared at the list, dipped a quill in ink and slowly scratched off *Experience a Perfect Kiss*. She had certainly done that in spades tonight. A perfect, *perfect* kiss that continued to haunt her mind and soul.

But no, she had pondered that enough. She wouldn't continue to do so, at least not right now. She looked at the rest of the list. She'd almost completed another item there, quite unexpectedly: *Fill My Dance Card.*

It was odd that doing no more than wearing a more revealing dress and fixing her hair fashionably had allowed all the same people who ignored her to suddenly see her. She just had to be something different and then she was interesting, which was disappointing.

It also put her to mind of what Sebastian had said to her on the terrace before he...

No, she wasn't going to think about the kiss, damn it.

He'd said she was being what she wasn't. Was he right? She thought about it, thought about all she'd done for Claudia's list. Often she'd actually felt *more* like herself when she was doing those things. Like she'd found some part of herself that she had buried or lost or forgotten.

Not when she was dancing tonight, perhaps, pursued by a gaggle of popinjays who didn't really care about knowing her, only taking their turn with someone who was popular for a moment. But when she was sitting in her parlor with Sebastian and giggling with him over naughty words, or swinging her fists in his transformed parlor, she had.

When she'd been kissed by him, she had. It hadn't felt wrong at all, or performative. It had felt magical, almost like she'd been asleep for all her life and he'd woken her up with just a touch.

She shook her head. It was entirely unfair that something that felt so right could very well ruin everything between them that she so cherished. That he might stay away from her. That he clearly thought he'd done something wrong if his words of apology before he left her alone in the darkness had been any indication. That he'd stop helping her with Claudia's list, even if he didn't know he was her secret partner in living her life more fully.

She blinked at sudden tears in her eyes. She'd already lost one friend, and she had few enough of them that she couldn't bear the idea of losing another.

But how could she stop it? In just two weeks' time he was supposed to join her brother and her for a week at their estate just outside of London for a small gathering. If she didn't do something quickly, what had happened between them would ruin that, too. Perhaps he wouldn't even come at all, and he was the only thing about that gathering that made it even the slightest bit bearable.

"I must talk to him," she said out loud, getting up from her table and pacing her chamber as she wrung her hands. "I must air this out in a place where we won't be interrupted and he cannot run away. But where?"

She returned to her table and stared once more at the list in Claudia's neat, even hand. One of the items stood out, almost glowed at her like a beacon that would somehow be the answer to her prayers.

Sneak Into a Gentleman's Home.

She caught her breath at the idea. If she did so, if she dared to sneak into his estate, he would have to listen to her, wouldn't he? She could refuse to leave until he did, if nothing else. They could hash out this madness between them and as a bonus, she could cross another item off her list.

"Thank you, Claudia," she murmured as she folded the list care-

JESS MICHAELS

fully and returned it to its safe spot in the jewelry box in the corner of her dressing table.

Then she blew out the candle and got into bed. She didn't think she had any better chance of sleeping than she'd had earlier, but at least she could lie in the softness of her pillows and try to figure out how to break into Sebastian's lair.

And what she could possibly say to him once she had.

CHAPTER 10

T he drink dangling from Sebastian's fingertips had been the same level for almost an hour, but he felt no drive to sip it. Just as he had felt no drive to fuck when he'd gone in nothing less than desperation to the Donville Masquerade and tried to find a willing lady to drive this haunting need into.

He'd found the willing party. Parties, actually. But he had not followed through, just as he hadn't the night he'd gone there with Delacourt. And now he was home, his mind swirling once again to the night before at the ball and his kiss on the terrace with Marianne.

He was beginning to accept the fact that he wanted her. *Truly* wanted her. Thinking of something else didn't help. Touching himself while he allowed every wicked fantasy didn't help. Nothing helped.

But he was still at a loss as to what to do about it.

"Sitting in the dark after midnight can't solve the problem, can it?" he muttered to himself as he slugged back the drink and set the glass on the edge of the desk.

He was about go upstairs to his chamber to continue his restless night and likely erotic dreams there when he heard the rap of something hitting his window.

He turned. Had he imagined the sound? Perhaps it was a bird hitting the glass or a—

Just then a small stone hit the glass a second time and he wrinkled his brow as he moved to look down. In the dim light he saw someone standing down below in his garden. Not just someone. As his eyes adjusted to the darkness, he realized it was Marianne.

He squeezed those same eyes shut then looked again, trying to determine if the madness of desire had conjured her like a phantom. But she was still there and she lifted her hand in a half wave to him.

He opened the window and leaned out. "What are you doing here?" he asked in a harsh whisper loud enough to carry to her.

She shrugged and he saw her mouth move but couldn't understand what she was saying. He held up a hand. "I'll come down, wait there."

He pivoted and rushed around to a parlor that led to the terrace and the stairs down to the garden. As he did so, he tried to calm his suddenly throbbing heart. Perhaps this was just another heated dream.

If so, that meant he could indulge in what he wanted all over. And if it was real then perhaps a talk with her and figuring out what the hell she was doing here would allow him to get over this once and for all.

She met him at the bottom of the stairs and her face was flushed.

"What are you doing here?" he asked again.

"May I come in?" she asked.

He sighed. That would be perfect, wouldn't it? Taking her inside where his servants might discover them in the middle of the night? Where he'd have plenty of beds and settees and rugs to tempt him to lay her out across them and…

He cleared his throat and motioned to the orangery across in one corner of the garden. That seemed a safer option.

"We'll have more privacy here," he suggested.

She followed him, he felt her there at his heels. Rather like the hounds of hell finally coming to collect him for his sins. Only they were lovely hounds of hell. Ones he didn't want to resist.

He opened the orangery door and they stepped into the warm, humid air. It was late enough in the season that all the trees were blossoming, and she took a deep breath of the sweetness.

"Oh, it's so lovely," she said, stepping forward to touch a blossom on one of the trees. "I so wish we had an orangery here in London where I could—"

Sebastian stepped forward and caught her wrist, turning her gently. "Marianne, what are you doing here? In the middle of the night? Unattended in my garden, throwing rocks at my window?"

She blinked and shifted, her discomfort as clear as his own. "I'm —I'm sorry. I was going to scale the wall, you see, and try to come in the window, but once I got here I didn't think the trellis would bear my weight. I didn't realize it was so flimsy. I don't know if this counts then, but I did want to see you and—"

He stepped back and interrupted her. "You were going to climb the trellis and try to come in through my window?" he repeated in disbelief.

She nodded slowly. "Y-Yes."

"Jesus," he grunted, and ran a hand through his hair at that thought. "Well, it's a good thing you didn't. The fall would have killed you."

"Yes, that was my assessment. Honestly, we are so often of a mind. Anyway, that's why I threw the rock when I saw your shadow moving around in your study."

He pinched the bridge of his nose and tried to remain calm. "You are talking about this as if it isn't something wildly unexpected and out of control. *And* you are avoiding my question, which makes me even more nervous. *What are you doing here, Marianne?*"

She sighed and clasped her hands before her. "We—we need to talk about what happened last night at the ball."

He pursed his lips. So it had come to this. "I see. And you couldn't have simply sent a note requesting a meeting in a more traditional way?"

She tilted her head. "Well, I thought—I thought you might not see me."

There was a lilt of pain to her voice that tugged his heart far more than it should. He stared at her, this woman who had stood along a wall being unnoticed for so many years. She'd been dismissed over and over again, and so she had assumed he would do the same.

Why wouldn't she? He had already done so over the years, he supposed. He'd called her friend and had ignored any of her plight or pain or fear or desires until she threw them up in his face and made him see what had always been standing right in front of him.

"Why wouldn't I see you?" he asked softly.

She shifted and a slight flush entered her cheeks. "You ran off in horror after we kissed, didn't you? You didn't even say goodbye."

"Marianne," he began.

But now she was the one who held up a hand, demanding she be allowed to continue. He noted how her fingers shook, saw how hard it was to make even this silent demand and so he shut his mouth and allowed her to speak instead.

"I don't know why you kissed me," she said. "But I don't want it to change things between us. That it would make you turn away from my brother or from…from me is my greatest fear. I want you to know that I'm not angry. I also have no expectation that the kiss meant anything to you, nor that you would ever wish to repeat it."

He stared now, that hunger he had felt for her for over twenty-four hours returning as his shock faded. She was back to her normal clothing, her hair was not done so fashionably as it had been the night before. Yet she was just as beautiful as she had been made up. He still felt the drive to touch her, to memorize the way her breath caught and her pupils dilated.

Even if he shouldn't.

"You think I wouldn't want to repeat it?" he asked, hearing the wicked drawl that always entered his voice when he was on the hunt.

She stared at him a long moment. "Why would you?"

In any other woman, that question would have been a playful part of a run and catch game. But Marianne meant it. She couldn't imagine he would want her. And that burned him down to his core. It made him want to be honest with her, even though he shouldn't. Even though it would only make this more complicated.

"All I've wanted to do since last night is kiss you," he said, closing the distance toward them at last. "Kiss you and kiss you. All I dreamed about was kissing you, and then much more."

Her lips parted, temptation in the way her tongue darted out to wet them. "You have?"

He nodded and then waited, watching her react. Her breath grew short, her gaze held his and she lifted a trembling hand to rest flat on his chest. He felt the weight of every finger and knew she likely felt the wild beat of his throbbing heart in return.

"Will you then?" she whispered, whimpered. "Please."

His own breathing ceased at the *please*. At the look of longing in her eyes that called so much to his own. He knew he wouldn't resist her, even if it burned the world down around him. He wanted to burn with it and her and there was no holding back anymore.

Sebastian felt so big as his arms came around Marianne. Just like before, his fingers bunched against her lower back, his head drifted down and she met his mouth with a hunger that she didn't fully understand.

Last night he had begun gently, but tonight there was none of that. It was as if they were picking up where they'd left off on the terrace. Like a breath separated one kiss from the other, rather than a night of tossing and turning and questioning.

She understood more now, so when his tongue met hers, she didn't hesitate. She lifted to him, tasting him as he'd tasted her and she reveled in the deep moan that escaped his lips when she did so. His fingers came into her hair, digging into the locks, loosening her pins slightly without allowing the hair to fall. He tilted her head and plundered more deeply as he backed her across the orangery to who knew where.

She felt the edge of a bench hit her knees and she allowed him to lower her to it. Only then did he part from her and stared down at her.

"Don't run away again," she said out loud, though she hadn't meant to.

"I should, but I can't." His breath was shockingly short and his expression wild. "I don't know what you're doing to me, Marianne. But I'm too weak to fight it now."

She hadn't even a moment to ponder the idea that she, a spinster, made a god like Sebastian feel weak. Before she could, he dropped to his knees before her and his mouth found hers again.

She wrapped her arms around his shoulders, clinging to him as the kiss grew as steamy as the orangery air. Now that he didn't have to hold her up, she felt his hands slide down her sides, her hips. He touched her thighs through the silky fabric of her gown and she sucked in a great gasp of air and pulled back.

"No?" he whispered, stilling his fingers.

"I came to you like a scarlet woman in the night," she whispered. "It's a little late for *no* now."

He shook his head and some of his wickedness turned gentle. "Oh no, my dear, there is never a moment that is too late for no. If you learn nothing else from me, take that lesson. No one should ever ignore your no. I'll stop if you don't want me to touch you like that."

She blinked at him, his handsome face even with hers, partially in the dark. He might look like a pirate, but he meant those words.

This man with a reputation for wickedness had no intention of *stealing* anything from her. Which meant she had to give it.

Terrifying.

"Do it again," she whispered. "It only surprised me."

He made a low chuckle and his fingers bunched against her skirt again, stroking her thighs through the satiny fabric.

"Why does it tingle?"

His voice was taut with tension as he choked out, "Because it makes you want. It sets your nerves on fire. It makes you long for more, even if you can't name it. I can give you more, Marianne. So much more than I should."

She didn't think, didn't ponder, she just nodded. "Yes. Please, please, yes."

He leaned forward and briefly his forehead touched hers. His breath was rough, his hands clenched against her thighs, and she heard him whisper, "God help me."

But when he pulled back and met her stare again, there was no hesitation in him. He licked his lips and then he inched her skirt up a fraction.

"Sebastian," she whispered.

He nodded slowly and inched farther. Now his hands went under the skirts, touching her stocking-clad legs with his bare hands. She felt his heat even through the fabric and she dropped her head back against the hardness of the bench.

She didn't know what he would do. It didn't matter. She wanted this, wanted him. Perhaps she had always known it might come to this if she went to him in the night. Perhaps she'd wanted it enough to risk his refusal.

His hands cupped her knees and he murmured, "Look at me."

She forced herself to do so and watched as he dropped his head to kiss first one knee then the other. His mouth was steamy and warm through the stockings and she gasped.

He smiled up at her as he gently pushed her knees apart, making her sit with her thighs open. He inched forward into that forbidden space and her skirt bunched between her legs as he did so.

"I like kissing you so much, Marianne," he purred. "You taste like heaven. I want to see if I'd like it as much somewhere else."

Her eyes went wide. "Wh-where?"

He slid his hands into her inner thighs. Above where her garters were tied, below where her chemise was bunched. Bare skin to wickedly bare skin.

"You're so soft, so wonderfully soft," he murmured, almost like a prayer she wasn't meant to hear.

But she did hear it and it set her body afire all the more. This man wanted her. Truly wanted her when he could have anyone else in the country, perhaps the world. She certainly couldn't picture the lady who could refuse him.

His thumbs pressed higher, hitting the edge of her chemise and the drawers beneath. He grunted out displeasure and then looked up at her. "I want to see you, Marianne. I want to see you and touch you and taste you until you are weak with it. Tell me yes. Please tell me yes."

CHAPTER 11

Marianne could barely think enough to answer Sebastian's plea as she stared down at him, perched between her legs so wickedly. He waited without pressing her and at last she found the ability to nod. Despite being dizzy with heated desire, she was unable to allow her modesty to override the momentum of this moment.

He pushed her gown and chemise up to her stomach and then he untied her drawers. They loosened and he tugged, sliding them from under her and tossing them away over his shoulder into the darkness.

Now she was bared to him, splayed like a reckless wanton, not a shy wallflower. But still, this didn't feel like she was parading around like someone she wasn't. No, this felt like glorious freedom and shocking fantasy rolled up in one.

He shook his head as he gently pressed his hands higher and his palms cupped her between the legs. This was wrong, so many people had said that to women over the years. Somehow it felt anything but. It felt hot, the pressure making her legs shake and her inner muscles squeeze against emptiness.

"I'm going to kiss you, Marianne," he whispered. "Just like I did your mouth. I'm going to kiss you right…" He leaned down, lewdly close to her spread body. "…here."

And then his mouth covered her in a place she had been taught to barely touch, in a place that had been preached as the property of some nameless, faceless future husband. But right now, with Sebastian's dark head between her legs, his fingers peeling her open wider, his tongue tracing her and tingles rushing through her entire body, she didn't feel like something to be owned. She felt like this magical man had opened her gilded cage and now she was flying.

She lifted into him on instinct, grinding up to find his firm tongue. He licked harder, grunting like it pleased him to taste every inch of her. He swirled across her entrance and past it, thrusting gently, then he withdrew and focused attention to some hidden, wonderful place that made her breath short.

"Oh, that feels good," she gasped out, gripping her hands against the edge of the bench seat.

"That's your clitoris," he murmured without lifting his mouth from her. His muffled voice reverberated through her and she hissed out pleasure. "And I want it to feel good. I want you to feel so good that you scream my name until you're hoarse. That you lose control of every part of your body. I want to feel your thighs grip my shoulders and your hands push my head in demand for more, Marianne."

She lolled her own head against the seat with every wicked word and the images they created, which merged with the sensation as he returned his full attention to that same place…clitoris, he'd called it. He swirled his tongue around it, lapping and licking a never-ceasing rhythm. Pleasure was mounting in her in a way she'd never experienced before. An excitement and a building pressure that bloomed between her legs. She dug a hand into his hair just as he'd told her he wanted, feeling his head bob against her as he chuckled against her.

"More," she moaned, no longer caring about propriety or wantonness or anything but his tongue on her flesh.

He didn't disappoint, for now he began to suck her, his tongue tapping as the pressure grew more and more. Her legs were no longer hers to control, she was only his marionette, and she danced in time to his ministrations until finally, in a burst of wetness and heat and unbelievable sensation, waves of pleasure rocked her.

She wailed because she could do nothing else, grinding in time to his endless torment as the pleasure edged out of control and her body quivered with sensations she'd never imagined were possible. His fingers dug into her thighs, his mouth moved faster against her and his panting breaths were hot against her as he forced every last drop of desire from her now-weak body.

Only when she went limp did he lift his face to look at her. The shadow of whiskers on his chin was damp with her juices, but it didn't seem to bother him. He licked his lips as he smiled up at her, triumphant as a cat who had caught himself a mouse and toyed with it until he was satisfied.

But after the briefest of moments, his smugness faded away. His expression drew down and she saw the same thing she'd seen on his face the previous night when he kissed her on the terrace: regret. The pain of it was worse for her this time because what they had shared was no mere kiss! This was something far more intimate and life-altering. Something that had changed her being down to her core.

"What is it?" she asked, shocked she could formulate words in a reasonably calm tone when her whole body was still tingling from pleasure.

He found her drawers and handed them over. Once she'd slid them on, he reached up and gently tugged her skirt back down to cover her, then got back to his feet and backed away. "Marianne, I am not a gentleman."

She wrinkled her brow as she sat up straighter. "Of course you are."

He stared up at the vaulted glass of the orangery ceiling and the stars that sparkled above them through it. "My actions aren't gentlemanly. My thoughts and designs when it comes to you are certainly not."

When it came to *her*. So she wasn't wrong. He didn't just want someone, anyone. Somehow, impossibly he wanted *her*.

In that moment, she felt a wave of emotion come over her just as the wave of pleasure had moments before. It was also just as revelatory because she knew, like a lightning bolt from the sky, that she was in love with him. She had always been in love with him, this man who had been like a star out of her reach for all the years she'd known him.

Tonight he'd come down from his orbit and she feared she would chase the feeling of his blinding light forever.

"Sebastian," she whispered.

He shook his head and his voice was rougher when he said, "Please. Your brother has only ever put one rule on our friendship. That I must never corrupt you."

Marianne rose to her feet in shock. "Phineas spoke to you about me in that fashion?" He hesitated and then nodded slowly. She stepped toward him and stopped when he tensed, his face twisting with more of that horrible regret. "Why would he ask that of you? Why would he ever think you'd want me?"

His brow wrinkled, as if he'd never considered that question before. "My reputation, I suppose."

She shook her head. "He couldn't have ever thought I was truly in danger from you."

"I think tonight proves otherwise."

"Oh, please. You aren't corrupting—"

"I am, I *have!*" His voice broke slightly and his expression became pained. "What I just did can be seen as nothing less. What is worse, I'll go even further if I'm given a chance. I won't be able to stop myself, just as I didn't stop myself tonight."

Her lips parted. It seemed her life was to be one surprise after another. "You mean you would...would..." She searched for a word and finally found it. "You would fuck me?"

He closed his eyes and swayed slightly at the very word he'd taught her weeks ago slipped from her lips. "Yes. I would most definitely *fuck* you, my lady. Until we were both spent and weak. Until you were ruined beyond repair. Until I was more of a cad than even my reputation would label me."

She shivered at the idea, still somewhat vague in her mind, but becoming clearer every time he touched her. She *wanted* what he suggested.

"But that would be between you and me, Sebastian," she whispered, stepping closer to him, feeling him tense when she took his hand and cupped it between her own. "No one's business but our own."

He stared down at her for a moment and she saw the waver in him. Then he lifted her hand to his lips and kissed her knuckles. "I cannot continue this," he said gently.

She tugged her hand away, disappointment marring the pleasure and the love and the warmth he had surrounded her in just a few moments before. "I see. Because of Finn."

"Yes." He ran a hand through his hair. "My family situation was so painful, Marianne."

"You think I don't know that?" she asked. "I was there just as he was. I saw your father's cruelty when you were young, Sebastian. I saw his dismissal of you and I watched it break your heart."

"Yes, you did." He drew a ragged breath. "Your kindness was one of the few balms on my soul in those days, Marianne. I haven't forgotten it. But Delacourt...*Finn*...he was the brother I...I..." He turned away.

She wrinkled her brow because she didn't understand why he'd break that sentence off. *The brother he'd never had* was clearly what he meant to say, but for some reason he withdrew. She watched him as he paced to one of the flowering trees and stand there, his shoulders tight and his hands clenched at his sides.

"He's all I have left now that my uncle is gone," he finished. "My only family, Marianne. I can't lose him. So I have to let you go. And because I care for you, because you do mean so much to me, I hope you can see that it's for *your* sake as much as my own."

He turned to look at her and she caught her breath. She hadn't realized how often Sebastian wore a mask, but now she saw the depth of his pain in the half-dark. She wanted to rush to him and demand and confess her own heart and try to force him to forget his hesitations.

But instead she pushed her shoulders back. "I'd never want to cause you pain, Sebastian. You are too dear to me for that."

His lips parted and his eyes widened and she felt the heat fill her cheeks. That was as close to telling him her heart as she would ever get.

"I won't bother you with this again," she said. "When we see each other, I'll never act differently. And I'd never tell Finn. I understand what you two mean to each other. How much you fill a void for each other. Now I'll leave you."

She moved toward the door to the orangery, but there she stopped, her hand shaking as she rested it on the handle. "Sebastian?"

"Yes?" he said, facing her.

"What we did...I want you to know it was wonderful. I never had any expectation that life could have so much beautiful...*color*. But you gave me that, not just tonight but in the last few weeks. It likely means little to you, but it meant everything to me. So, thank you."

He stared at her, his hands flexing at his sides. When he didn't reply, she inclined her head. "Goodnight."

"Goodnight," he said softly as she exited the orangery and fled across the garden back toward the gate where she'd snuck in and the horse that awaited her in the narrow lane behind his house.

It hadn't been the night she'd wanted, even though she couldn't exactly label what she'd hoped for when she brought herself to the man's window. But she'd recognized her heart and surrendered a part of her body. She'd gained something magnificent and lost something precious all the span of a heartbeat.

And she feared life could never, would never, be the same after that. Even if she had to pretend it was.

∾

Sebastian reentered his house, his entire body shaking. What he had done with Marianne still lingered on every inch of his body. But what she'd said he feared would be a part of his thoughts for the rest of his life.

He'd spent his adult life in dissipation. Oh, he wasn't entirely irresponsible—he took care of those who needed his attention, like his servants and tenants. But he tried to studiously avoid any connection that would require he...try. Trying was terrifying. The idea that he could let someone down haunted him.

But Marianne had scrambled everything he thought of himself in a moment when she'd said she hadn't expected life to have color. That he had put that color into her world.

The idea that *he* could do that for her was...magical. It puffed up his chest, it made him want to find more ways to do it. It made him want to be different than the way he presented himself to those around him.

Which was reason enough to stop toying with Marianne, even without the added issue of Delacourt and his edict for Sebastian all those years ago. He couldn't be the color in Marianne's world. He would let her down if he tried. She would break and he would hate himself more than he already did. And so would her brother.

He had to forget her taste, forget the feel of her arching beneath him, moaning for more. He had to forget her kindness and sweetness and the way she looked at him like he could pull the moon down and give it to her. Like she could make him want to.

He had to forget it all and then he would survive, as he'd always fought to survive.

CHAPTER 12

Delacourt's fist slid across Sebastian's chin and it was only that his friend held back that kept him from being knocked on his arse in the middle of the ring.

"Jesus," Delacourt barked. "Keep your hands up, you're acting like you've never done this before."

Sebastian lifted a wrapped hand to indicate he needed a moment and walked back to the corner of the ring. They were at their boxing club, Ripley's, as was their normal Wednesday activity, but he wasn't focusing. He swept up a towel and wiped a bit of sweat from his bare chest. He had to get his mind right or Delacourt was correct. He was going to get hurt.

"What is wrong with you?"

He turned to find Delacourt standing over his shoulder, rubbing his own chest with a towel. He looked both annoyed and concerned.

"Distracted," Sebastian said with a shrug. "I can't seem to stop being distracted."

"Over anything in particular?" Delacourt asked.

Sebastian looked at him as he folded the towel over the ring rope and walked back to the center of the sparring area. "Nothing I wish to discuss."

"Hmmm." Delacourt followed. "Seems you and my sister suffer the same affliction."

Now Sebastian tensed, even as he tried to keep his voice unaffected. "What? Distraction?"

"Yes. Though I suppose Mari is much more often troubled in her thoughts and even more so since the death of her friend." He sighed.

Sebastian almost did the same. He didn't want to hear that Marianne suffered, but there was a part of him that was happy they were both caught up in the same swirl. At least he wasn't alone in his unwanted thoughts.

"I hope the country party will lift her spirits," Delacourt said as they set their feet again to continue their sparring. "And yours. Our carriage will pick you up Saturday morning around ten, if that is agreeable."

Sebastian frowned as he threw a punch, which Delacourt easily blocked. "I've been meaning to talk to you about that. I think it would be better if I rode my own mount out."

Honestly, it would be better if he didn't go at all, but he couldn't do that. He loved going to the yearly party that Delacourt and Marianne hosted at the end of each summer. And if he were honest with himself, he wanted to see her. He hadn't seen her in two weeks. It gnawed at him. If he could go to this party and be appropriate, then perhaps it would put them back on the road to their old friendship. He wouldn't lose her.

Delacourt paused and lowered his hands. "Why?"

That was a loaded question, but Sebastian shrugged. "I have some things to do and I don't want to keep you from your preferred arrival time."

Delacourt wrinkled his brow but nodded. "Very well, it's your decision, of course. I think it will be a smashing party. You need the break. So do I."

Now Sebastian tilted his head, his own torments forgotten as he saw raw frustration on his friend's face. "What do you need a break from?"

Delacourt pursed his lips and his gaze turned distant for a moment. "Irritations that are not worth discussing. Come, lift those hands, I need to box out some of this discomfort."

Sebastian did as he'd asked, but as they returned to their sparring, he couldn't help but wonder what would come of all these secrets the three of them were keeping from each other. And what would happen if he allowed his desires for Marianne to overwhelm him at the country party.

He just had to control himself.

"Marianne?"

Marianne jolted and looked up from her tea to find her brother watching her with concern in his stare. She forced a smile. "My apologies, Finn. I'm such a featherbrain as of late."

"You've been distracted," he said slowly. "For almost two weeks, yes."

She flinched. Two weeks. Finn had unknowingly pinned the exact date of when she'd gone to Sebastian. When he'd done such wicked things with his tongue that had haunted her dreams ever since. When he'd told her he wouldn't ever choose her over his friendship with her brother.

"I'm simply busy with party preparations," she said, pointing to the papers they had been working on together during their tea. "We leave in so short a time—I want to ensure everything is perfect."

His brow wrinkled. "We've done this party every year for I can't recall how long and it's always wonderful, Mari. You needn't trouble yourself so much that it keeps you up at night."

She took a slow sip of her tea so he wouldn't note how his statement affected her. "Who says I'm up at night?"

"Aunt Beulah mentioned hearing you wandering the halls when I took her to church last week," Finn said. "The day you had a headache."

"She cannot hear when I ask her to pass the tea, but she has no problem listening to me go to the library late at night to fetch a book?" Marianne said with a forced laugh.

She got a half-smile in return. "Well, she'll enjoy being on her own while we're gone. I think she intends to call on all her friends."

"Yes, and Cousin Fiona is coming, I believe," Marianne said absently as she looked at a sketch of the guest rooms in the estate outside of London. Names were written in the boxes representing them. Sebastian's was there, in her own hand, in the chamber closest to the family quarters. Four doors down from her own.

"…won't be going with us in the carriage as usual."

Finn's voice pierced her thoughts again and she jerked her head up. "I'm sorry, what was that?"

"You remain distracted," he said with a shake of his head. "An affliction that Ramsbury shares, it seems. He told me when I met with him yesterday that he didn't intend to ride with us to the estate."

She drew in a breath. She and Sebastian had been studiously avoiding each other for weeks, but the three of them always rode out to the estate in the carriage together for this gathering. She'd actually been looking forward to it, hoping that the time together with her brother as chaperone would help them get some of their old friendship back.

"Did he give a reason?"

"Not a good one," Finn said with a shake of his head. "He's been out of sorts lately. I've tried to determine why. Perhaps it's trouble with a lady."

Marianne clenched her hands in her lap. "Well, that would fit his personality, wouldn't it?"

Her brother laughed again. "It would. Or it did but he isn't—" He cut himself off. "Forgive me, these are not topics to discuss with my sister."

"He still intends to come, though?" she asked, hating the lilt of desperation to her tone. "He hasn't rejected the invitation outright?"

"He's coming," her brother said. "And I think we'll all enjoy the respite. London seems too...close this year. Too hot."

There was something in her brother's tone that drew Marianne's attention to him. He had a troubled line to his lips, but he didn't give her a chance to question him about it.

"Now I'm off to my club. Must meet with a few gentlemen before we depart. Thank you again for the company and all the assistance. I do appreciate you." He pressed a quick kiss to her cheek and then he was gone, thundering out of her drive a few moments later.

Marianne sat staring at what remained of her tea, her breath a bit shorter. Then she got up and rang her bell. When Adams appeared, she said, "Will you fetch me something to write with and ask a footman to prepare to deliver it immediately?"

"Yes, my lady, of course."

After he departed, she returned to the table and pushed aside her drink and all the papers she had been studying with Finn. Right now she had more pressing matters to attend to. Ones she could no longer pretend away.

Sebastian had received many letters from Marianne over the years. Invitations to suppers, messages of thanks for some small kindness, larger letters of condolence that he still kept in the drawer of his desk, along with the gloves she had forgotten when she came to box at his home what felt like a lifetime ago.

Never had one been so curt as the one he'd received half an hour before. The one practically burning a hole in his pocket as he rode onto her drive.

I need to see you. Now.
Marianne.

Two lines and a signature, nothing more. And yet he felt her frustration in every word.

"Good, then she is matching my own," he muttered as he swung off the horse and gave over the reins to her servant. He was halfway to the door when it opened and revealed the lady herself.

He stopped on the stairs to look at her. Had pale green always been her color? It was really lovely on her, with the sunshine coming down on her like a beacon. She almost looked like a wood sprite. Were those supposed to be wicked or good? He couldn't recall.

"I'm pleased you came," she said.

He shook off his unexpected thoughts and tried to behave as he normally would by forcing a smile. She didn't return it, but ducked her gaze from his as she motioned him inside.

"I'm surprised to be greeted directly by you."

She was already turning away to guide him down the hallway to a parlor. "Yes, Adams was equally taken aback when I demanded I meet you in his stead. But here we are. None of us are acting ourselves of late."

He pressed his lips together and entered the room behind her. She stayed at the door as he passed and surprised him by pushing it shut.

He pivoted. "Marianne—"

She held up a hand. "Don't worry yourself, Sebastian, I have no intention of doing anything to violate the terms of our earlier agreement to distance ourselves. But I heard something from my brother today that I had to address with you in person."

He shifted. "And what was that?"

"Finn says you shall not ride with us to Garringford Corners."

He smiled slightly at the name of the siblings' small estate just outside London and memories of all the happy times they'd spent there over the years. Marianne didn't return the expression, but remained singularly focused on the topic at hand. "Is that true?"

"I'm surprised he would say something about that, it's meaningless." A lie, but he continued, "I intend to ride behind later in the day. I won't arrive much after you two do."

"Exactly why he mentioned it, I assume, as it goes against our habit of how we normally travel to this yearly gathering," she said, folding her arms. The action lifted her breasts a little, a distraction he tried to ignore.

"I see," he said softly. "And what is your fear?"

"You pretend you don't know?" She moved forward but brought herself up short before she got too close. That was probably for the best because he wasn't certain he could meter his response at the moment. "You're acting out of character. Don't you fear he'll recognize that I'm the reason?"

"Does he notice *you* acting out of character?" he asked.

She caught her breath. "Of course he doesn't. He thinks any change in my behavior has only to do with Claudia's death. But I mean less to him than you do."

He drew back at that statement. "That isn't true. You must know that you mean the world to him."

"I'm a difficulty he must bear. A disappointment, I'm sure," she insisted, and for a moment all her pain was clear. Pain he wanted to ease with such a power that it was almost frightening. He pushed aside his baser desires and moved on her.

He caught both her hands and held them to his chest. "You could *never* be a disappointment, Marianne. Not to him, not to—" He cut himself off and released her. He ran a hand through his hair. "I've known your brother for more than half my life and he has never spoken of you with anything but love and affection. He adores you."

"And yet you don't think he'd notice any change to me. Nor to you."

"He has his own distractions," Sebastian said with a slight shake of his head as he thought of Finn's faraway expressions the past little while.

Now she straightened. "Finn? What do you mean? Is he well?"

"Yes," Sebastian said. "He won't speak to me about it in detail, but I can see it in his face. So I don't think you have to worry about your brother suddenly noticing that we don't want to stand near each other or that I might not travel with you because I worry that I'll—" Once again he cut himself off. It wasn't fair to say more when he had demanded they stop this madness between them. "Was that all you needed?"

She stared up at him and he couldn't help but notice all the lovely lines of her face. Strange that he hadn't ever been so taken in by them in years past and now all he could do was analyze every little twitch and movement of them.

"Yes." She shifted. "Except..."

He smiled slightly. "*Except?*"

"Do you really not wish to stand near me?" she said. "Is that how far this has come?"

He sighed. "I'll gladly stand beside you, Marianne. Like you, I don't want what we shared to ruin our friendship. It means a great deal to me. I simply must be more careful until this...this desire fades."

She nodded. "Well, you know best when it comes to desire. If you say it will fade, then I believe you."

His hand fluttered at his side, and for a moment he almost let himself defy all their agreements and touch her. God, how he wanted to do just that. To touch her and then never stop touching her. Not until they both had their fill of pleasure.

But he had to be stronger than that. He stepped back instead. "It must. I'll see you at Garringford Corners in a few days. Good day, Marianne."

He pivoted on his heel and strode from the parlor, from her

home. He could feel her watching him and when he mounted his horse he gave a quick glance over his shoulder to find her at the window, doing just that. As he rode away he drew a shuddering breath. There had to be a way to overcome this.

There just had to be.

CHAPTER 13

As Marianne stood at the edge of the parlor, watching her brother and so many of his good friends as they laughed and chatted, she felt the keenest sting of missing Claudia. She had invited her dear friend to Garringford Corners for this gathering a few times. She had only convinced shy Claudia to come once and then she had marveled at how Marianne could bear all the loud, boisterous men.

"They hardly see me," she had responded at the time, and they'd gone to get their tea without anyone even noticing they'd left.

But today it was different. There was no Claudia to cling to, giggling over the other guests. And she was no longer unseen. Several of Finn's friends occasionally looked her way with a smile or a tilt of their heads.

And there was always Sebastian, who was across the room at the fireplace, chatting with another gentleman. His gaze flitted to her over and over and she tried not to blush every time he did.

"Lady Marianne."

She jolted as she was approached by Mr. Lanford. He hadn't been invited to this event by her brother before, so she wasn't exactly certain why he was here now, but he'd been kind enough to her at the Brighthollow ball and she wasn't sorry to see him.

"Mr. Lanford, I'm so glad you could join us."

"You and your brother are kind to invite me," he said. "Your estate is lovely, as are you."

She glanced down at herself. Since that night at the ball, her maid, Hannah, had been altering her dresses, making all of them a little more daring. She still wasn't entirely accustomed to the lack of lace concealing her collarbones yet, but it was becoming less uncomfortable with every day.

"Thank you," she said, and felt the heat in her cheeks at the compliment. She wasn't used to receiving those, either. "And we do enjoy it here. We're close enough to London to make it convenient and far enough away to have some little peace. Not like Delacourt, which is days away by carriage."

He nodded. "I do agree that this close-in estate is heavenly. We can shoot in the morning and be out to some of the hells by night." He stopped himself. "Forgive me, I should not speak of such things with you."

She shook her head. Her ears had actually perked up when he said the hells. Playing faro in one of those mysterious places was on Claudia's list, after all, and she knew nothing of them. Since she didn't have Sebastian as a guide anymore, this was an opportunity to find out more in a natural way.

"Not at all. I've always been interested in hearing more about those places. They also call it the underground, yes? Are they truly under the ground? How would that work?"

He laughed, but it wasn't unkind. "No, my lady. Just secret. Well, an open secret, since we all know about them. Clubs where people can wager and drink and enjoy themselves a little more freely."

"And there is one close by?"

"Many are in the heart of the city, closer to where you live when you're in Town. But there are a few on the outskirts." He stepped a little closer. "Are you truly curious?"

She examined him carefully. He had a kind enough face and had not been untoward with her. "I...am," she admitted. "I don't suppose a lady such as myself might be invited along."

He glanced over his shoulder toward her brother. "Delacourt might not like it."

"I'm sure he wouldn't," she said. "But I am an independent woman, you know."

"You are, indeed," Lanford said with a sly smile. "I could escort you if you'd truly like to observe such a place."

Her eyes widened. "Would you? Oh, that would be delightful, Lanford, thank you. When?"

"Tonight?" he suggested. "After supper? If you can slip out, that is."

"Easily," she said with a laugh. "I fade into the woodwork here during these things."

"I doubt that," he said. "Excellent. Then meet me in the foyer at say, ten? I'll arrange the rest."

"I will," she said with smile before he nodded and excused himself.

When he was gone, she drew a long breath. This man was offering her a lifeline without even knowing it. If she put her focus back on Claudia's list, that would keep her mind off Sebastian and all the things she couldn't have when it came to him.

And since he wasn't even looking at her anymore as he chatted with his friends, that was for the best.

Sebastian didn't like feeling out of sorts and yet that was all he'd been since his arrival at Garringford Corners that afternoon. Normally, he found respite here with Delacourt and their friends, with Marianne. But since his arrival he had felt only frustration. Worse, he knew the cause. He could see it as Marianne stood across the parlor talking with some of the other gentlemen as they all shared an after-supper drink. He pressed his lips together and turned to where Delacourt had just finished a conversation with another of their friends and now stood nursing his drink.

"I say, doesn't it bother you that your sister is center of attention to that...that pack of jackals?"

Delacourt blinked and looked across the room. "You consider Mr. Lanford and the Marquess of Millington to be jackals? One is nothing but a gentleman and the other is married."

"Marriage hasn't stopped many a man, and you know it. And as for Lanford, he is nothing but a gentleman on the *surface*," Sebastian huffed.

"Are you saying you know something untoward about the man?" Delacourt asked, his grip tightening around his glass.

Sebastian briefly considered lying, giving an answer that would put Delacourt on guard with Lanford. But then he shook his head. "I...no. I hardly know him. That's what I'm saying. He could be any kind of man. Why did you invite him anyway? He never ran with our group in school."

Delacourt shrugged and he was back to the nonchalant disconnection from the subject. "I thought Marianne might like him to be here. She mentioned he was friendly to her at the Brighthollow ball a few weeks ago."

"She *mentioned* him?" Sebastian repeated, feeling the flare of his nostrils at that fact. He hated that he was jealous. He was never jealous.

"In passing." Delacourt faced him full on now. "What is wrong with you? Marianne always plays hostess at these things. She's bound to draw the polite attention of the attendees."

Sebastian folded his arms. "I simply find it odd that you are so protective of her around me, but not around them."

Delacourt arched a brow. "It seems to me that *you* are the one who could hurt her more. If you don't know why, then you have no observational skills."

He turned and walked away and Sebastian stared, stunned by

that statement. He looked at Marianne again. She was laughing and her face was lit up the same way he'd seen it a dozen times over the years when she stared up into *his* eyes.

Delacourt couldn't mean that Marianne had feelings for him. The desire, yes, of course. That was a recent development. Or was it? Now he couldn't be certain.

He gulped for air as Lanford separated himself from Marianne at last and headed his way. Marianne had turned her attention to the marquess now and was continuing to talk, though with far less animation than she had with Lanford.

"Ah, Ramsbury," Lanford said with a friendly smile when he reached Sebastian. "Quite a gathering, isn't it?"

"Yes," Sebastian grunted, making the barest effort to be civil. "Seems you're enjoying yourself greatly with Lady Marianne."

Lanford looked across the room at her. "She's a fascinating little creature, isn't she? A wallflower, but something more is there under the surface."

Sebastian said nothing and dropped his gaze to the drink he gripped in his white-knuckled hand. "Indeed."

"I say, a few of us are going to Hedgewig's tonight around ten to gamble. Will you join us?"

Sebastian lifted his head. Hedgewig's was a shabby little hell just two miles from Delacourt's estate. Normally he didn't mind the place—it wasn't the worst, nor the best of its ilk. He had gone there plenty of times over his many visits here.

But tonight he had no interest. In fact, he was pleased this man would just *go away*. Perhaps it would give Sebastian a chance to speak alone with Marianne. Only to make certain that she understood what a man like Lanford was capable of expecting, even if he presented himself as a gentleman to her.

"No," he said. "I appreciate the offer, but I'll decline this time."

Lanford shrugged. "Suit yourself, Ramsbury. Ah, I see Mr. Pettigrew motioning my way. Excuse me."

Sebastian nodded him away and then drew a deep breath. Good, now he had a plan. If Lanford's group was to depart at ten for their outing, he would find Marianne by ten-thirty and speak to her. Settle things with her. Protect her. That was all this was about, after all. Protecting her.

There was nothing else to it at all.

~

Sebastian stepped into the library at precisely ten-thirty and expected Marianne to be there. After all, that was her habit when she came to this estate. Read before bed for precisely three-quarters of an hour.

How did he know that? He couldn't recall when he'd learned it or how he'd saved the knowledge over the years. But there it was.

Only when he came into the chamber, the room was empty. Not even the fire was lit. He wrinkled his brow. She had excused herself just before ten, so he had assumed...

He turned and nearly ran into one of the maids as she came up the hallway.

"Excuse me," he said as she stepped out of his way with a bent head. He looked more closely at her. "You are Lady Marianne's maid, are you not?"

The young woman lifted her gaze. "I am, my lord. May I help you?"

"Perhaps. I'm looking for her. Do you know where she might be?"

"She retired to her chamber a while ago," the maid said. "But she hasn't yet called for me to help her ready for bed, so she's likely reading or sewing there. Would you like me to find her?"

Sebastian's mouth went dry at the idea of Marianne in her bedroom. Alone. He shook the thought away. "Er, no. If she's retired, I wouldn't want to trouble her. I'll speak to her tomorrow. Thank you."

The maid curtsied slightly and then walked away. He waited a moment, then cursed beneath his breath as he started toward the stairs. He *would* have this conversation with Marianne tonight. Before she allowed herself to get caught up in what might be a foolish friendship. At least he had to help her keep her eyes open, didn't he?

Only that didn't feel like his purpose as he stepped up to her door and knocked. He waited a moment, but there was no answer. Was it possible she'd fallen asleep? He knocked again, this time a bit louder. Still there was no reply.

He was about to step away, to go look for her again, when he bumped the door and it opened slightly. His breath caught. Entering her private rooms was not only rude, but it was scandalous. The exact kind of thing that could inspire her brother's rightful rage or even harm her reputation. What he *should* do was close the door firmly and either send for the maid to fetch her or just wait until morning to talk to her.

"Probably would be best for me, as well," he muttered to himself as he stared at that cracked door.

And then he pushed it open and stepped inside.

Although he'd known Marianne for as many decades as he'd known her brother, he'd never seen her private chamber. Of course he wouldn't. He'd never found himself curious about it, either, but now he stared around the antechamber and his breath caught.

It was lovely. She had decorated it beautifully, with unique art and dried flowers. There were sketches framed on the walls, too, ones he thought she might have done herself over the years. He vaguely recalled her sometimes having a blank book for that purpose when they hiked around the estate in the summer. And there were piles of books everywhere, on almost every surface. The room looked lived in and treasured, a little feminine escape from a world where she mostly spent time with her brother or friends like the ones gathered here this week.

"Marianne?" he called out as he drew a finger across a table that contained stationery, quills, a wax seal for letters. He recognized her scrawling, messy handwriting on one of the pages, though he didn't read the words. He only thought of all the letters she'd written to him over the years and smiled.

"Marianne?" he repeated as he came closer to the door across the antechamber. The one that led to her bedroom. He briefly pictured her curled up on her bed, dozing. Pictured crossing to her and waking her with a kiss. Where would a kiss lead in the dark quiet of a private room? Would he be able to stop himself from losing control if she wrapped her arms around his neck and...

He shook his head and opened the door to the adjoining bedroom. "Marianne?"

Only there was no one inside. Her bed was perfectly made, her fire burned low. There was no candle or lamp lit to ease her reading or drawing or sewing. She wasn't there.

He definitely should have left then, but he found himself violating her privacy further than he already had by stepping fully into the room. Again, it was a beautiful chamber that contained all the depths of Marianne's personality. There was a cozy chair by the fire decorated in a pretty woven fabric of pinks and yellows and blues and more books beside it, as well as a half-finished blanket she must have been crocheting.

She brought the things she loved into these four walls, including a few miniatures on a dressing table by the window. He moved toward them and smiled at the picture of her brother staring back at him. This was a likeness made just after he'd inherited his title. There was one of the two siblings together as well, Marianne's lips just barely smiling like she was trying not to laugh and Delacourt's eyes slightly cast toward her.

There was a larger likeness of their parents on the table. Unlike the other portraits, there was no warmth to them. But then again, that reflected their reality just as much, if Sebastian recalled correctly. The late earl and his wife had had a volatile relationship. One that had led to the countess's early demise, which had been whispered about endlessly. The scandal had cut short and ultimately damaged Marianne's coming. And her father's drinking and loud, uncouth cruelty to everyone he had encountered in the following years had done nothing to help her recover from that loss.

As he picked up the silver-framed painting to look at it, he realized that there was another hidden behind it and the discovery of it made his knees wobble a little. It was him. His miniature was placed here with the rest, a very old piece done when he was still in school. How had she even gotten this? And why had she kept it?

He placed the portrait of her parents back where it had belonged and caught his breath, which was suddenly short. He didn't know why or how she had the picture. More to the point, he shouldn't care about it either. He had come into this room without her permission and he didn't want to see anything more of her internal life.

He was about to turn and flee when he noticed a large sheet of heavy vellum that was folded haphazardly next to the collection of portraits in front of a pretty jewelry box with an intricate design of brass overlayed on it.

He didn't recognize this handwriting, and for a moment his heart leapt. What if it was from an admirer? Even Lanford? Would that explain Marianne's absence from the places Sebastian believed she should be?

He picked it up, hating himself even more for these betrayals after betrayals he was committing against her. But it didn't stop him from unfolding the sheet.

Only to find that it wasn't a passionate letter from a lover at all. It was a list entitled *Daring to Live Before I Die, Things to Do.*

Sebastian's nearly toppled himself over as he rushed to the fire to read the message more clearly in the light there. Die? Was Marianne dying? No, this wasn't in her hand. And it didn't seem to be a man's hand either, for it was delicate and neat and decidedly feminine. And then he recalled her friend's death. Claudia. She'd been ill, hadn't she? Perhaps knowing she would die.

Was this *her* list?

His gaze darted from one item to another, not even in the correct order in his panic, and his eyes widened:

Learn to Play Billiards.

Say Something Shocking.

Learn What Naughty Words Mean and Use Them in a Sentence.

The last one was crossed out in a different ink then it had been written in. He tensed as he thought about that day in Marianne's home when he'd taught her all those naughty words and watched her sweet mouth form them as his body became edgier and more focused on her. He pushed those thoughts away and continued to read the list:

Go to a Party Uninvited.

Wear Something Daring.

Again, that one was crossed off and he pulled the list to his chest and thought of Marianne in her beautiful gown at the Brighthollow ball. The one that had drawn every man's attention in the room, including his own. The one that had made her look so intoxicating that he hadn't been able to stop himself from kissing her as he asked...

As he asked her why she had been behaving so strangely recently. When she'd denied him an answer.

"Marianne," he groaned as he began to realize exactly why that might be. He returned his attention to the list:

Be Unchaperoned with a Man.

That item had a question mark next to it and in Marianne's hand, for he knew it instantly, it read: *Does Sebastian count?*

He stared. The annotations on the list, the lines through the items, those were in Marianne's hand. He looked further to verify:

Get Drunk. Crossed off.

Find Out What Boxing is All About. Crossed off.

Experience a Perfect Kiss.

His breath caught as he saw Marianne had crossed that item off, only the line was shaky, as if she'd been trembling when she did it.

The perfect kiss. The kiss they'd shared on the terrace, perhaps. It had been a perfect kiss. Powerful and heated and passionate.

He continued to scan the list and saw the words *love affair*, but before he could read that further, he was drawn to another item, this one with one more of Marianne's notes beside it.

Play Faro in a Hell.

His stomach clenched because next to that item, she'd written: *Mr. Lanford.*

"Christ," he muttered, tossing the list aside on the table and pivoting toward the door. She was going to the hell with Lanford. After so much time since he'd last seen her, she was likely already *at* the hell. And there were those kinds of places where a lady wouldn't stand out, but Hedgewig's wasn't one of them. Marianne didn't belong there.

And he needed to get to her as soon as possible so that she didn't get herself into too much trouble.

CHAPTER 14

Marianne had spent many a pleasant hour playing faro and other card games with friends, but most especially Claudia. And she found, as she sat at the table surrounded by strange men and women, smoke clouding the air around her, drinks flowing freely, that she was benefiting from the practice. She collected her winnings yet again with a laugh as the next event began.

While the cards were shuffled, she glanced around the room. She had pictured a great many things while hearing about hells and the underground in whispered tones from people who thought she was too innocent to hear them.

But once inside, she found it was just a large parlor, kind of like a tearoom in Bath, only with more men and louder arguments and somewhat raucous behavior from the visitors.

She jerked her attention back to the matter at hand as the banker began to lay out the cards before him. Only she saw something that caught her eye. The man to his closest left was slipping his gaze toward the banker's shoulder. Toward the cards.

"Excuse me, sir," she said, motioning to the banker. "I believe the gentleman on the left can see."

The man in question jerked his gaze toward her, his bleary eyes growing wide. "I beg your pardon, chit?"

"Perhaps you didn't mean to," she said as the others at the table began to stare at her and uneasiness rose from deep within her. "It's —it's so easy to accidentally do just that when directly beside the banker."

The banker twisted in his seat and started waving his hand. "What did I tell you, Wilcox? Over and over, you lousy cheat?"

"I weren't cheating!" the man she'd accused said. "That little whore is lying!"

Marianne gasped at the nasty accusation and pushed her chair back slightly as the accused, Wilcox got up and leaned across the table toward her. "Do you know who I am, bitch? Do you know what I can do?"

Fear streaked through her, its cold hand chilling every part of her body. She'd never been spoken to in such a manner before and she realized how badly she had miscalculated this interaction in her naivety. Slowly she stood and held up her hands to block her face, just as Sebastian had taught her when they sparred. But she didn't think one of her punches could stop this man. Perhaps, though, she could still calm the angry bull who looked ready to charge.

"I wasn't trying to cause trouble, only to play a fair game, sir."

"And we'll have one. You're banned, Wilcox!"

The banker lifted a hand to motion for someone to come over, likely to escort the angry man out, but before he could, Wilcox lunged at her. She staggered back, crashing into her own chair as she covered her head with her hands and waited to be struck. Only it didn't happen because before he could reach her another man shoved his way between them and pushed the cheat so hard that he stumbled backward and fell across the table behind him.

There was a great deal of shouting and then a true fight began, sending everyone from her table rushing to join the battle. She looked up to see who her savior was and felt all the color drain from her cheeks as she realized it was Sebastian. He was here, and he was glaring down at her as he grabbed her hand and began to drag her away from the melee that had begun.

"What were you thinking, Marianne?" he hissed.

She could formulate no answer for she had never seen Sebastian like this before. His bright eyes had no teasing light in them, but were dark with emotion and his fingers gripped hers with almost desperation as he pulled her across the room.

"Answer me!" he insisted, moving her ever closer to the door.

Behind them, Mr. Lanford suddenly rushed up, his face red and his breath short. "Great God, Ramsbury, I didn't think you were going to join us!"

Sebastian turned an even more thunderous expression on him. "Outside with you, too," he grunted, and motioned toward the door.

Chaos reigned behind them as he maneuvered them outside where people were either streaming out of the building to escape the punches being thrown or rushing in to take part in the fray.

Once Sebastian had gotten them to where the carriages were parked, away from some of the cacophony of the hell, he released Marianne and grabbed Lanford by the lapels. As Marianne jerked her hand up to cover her mouth, Sebastian slammed him into the side of the closest carriage.

"What the fuck were you thinking, you absolute twat?" he said, too quiet and too close to Lanford's face.

The other man swallowed, sweat breaking out on his brow. "I-I-I—"

"You think this place is a for a *lady?*" Sebastian continued. "Do you think that the Earl of Delacourt would be pleased that you took his innocent sister to a hell where a fight would break out just for looking in the wrong direction?"

"I-I thought it would be a laugh," Lanford managed to gasp out. "I was there, wasn't I? To-to protect her if need be."

"Were you?" Sebastian pushed him harder against the vehicle and then dropped him into a heap at his feet. "Because I didn't see you anywhere near her. I saw you flirting with a lightskirt across the room while Marianne nearly got assaulted by some drunken card cheat."

He pivoted toward Marianne, his eyes flashing and his hands trembling. "What carriage did you come in?" he asked, his tone sharp and hard.

"I-It was Mr. Lanford's carriage," she whispered, tears stinging her eyes.

"Where?" Sebastian barked, turning back to Lanford.

Lanford pointed a few down the row. "That one," he said. "The blue one."

"Good. My horse is being held by the groom just there. You will follow us home on him. And you will keep your poxy mouth shut about all of this, do you understand?"

Lanford nodded as he got up and brushed the dirt from the muddy drive off his trousers as best he could. "Y-Yes, my lord."

Without another word, Sebastian caught Marianne's elbow and drew her forward again. This time he stopped at the same carriage she had taken to the hell not an hour ago and yanked the door open.

"Take us back to Delacourt's estate," he growled at the stunned-looking servant, who cast a quick glance at his muddy master before Sebastian yanked the carriage door shut and locked them into the darkness together.

Lanford must have indicated that the driver follow Sebastian's order, for not a moment passed before they began to move. Sebastian said nothing, just sat across from her, arms folded, breathing heavily in the oppressive quiet of the carriage.

Marianne shifted and the shock of what had happened began to fade. "How did you know I was here?" she asked.

He was quiet a moment, but the mood in the carriage shifted again, this time she felt...guilt. He almost seemed *guilty* even though she had been the one to do something outrageous.

"Sebastian," she said.

He turned his face toward the window. "Lanford invited me and

I intended not to go, but changed my mind. When I arrived, I saw you."

She gripped her hands in her lap at the dismissiveness of that statement. "And so you decided to humiliate me in front of a room full of strangers and probably neighbors, not to mention Mr. Lanford?"

He leaned forward and a shaft of moonlight hit his face, creating hard angles. "So worried about Lanford's opinion, are you?"

"Why would you care?" she asked, and the fear she had felt so keenly earlier began to transform into something harsher. It turned to anger. "You made it clear in London that you have no interest in me. Why would it possibly matter if I valued the opinion of some other gentleman?"

"A gentleman." He let out an ugly laugh. "It isn't *gentlemanly* to escort a lady to a place like that and then not closely take care of her well-being."

"Ah, so the problem was not me going there, it was him not watching me like I was a petulant child." She shook her head. "I have enough over-protection from my brother, Sebastian, I don't need it from you."

"It seems you do. And the problem, my dear, *is* you going there because you don't know how to protect yourself. You don't know what to look for in a crowd of half-drunk men who expect the women are willing...more willing then I think you'd wish to be with a stranger. You don't know how not to start a fight over a cheat at faro."

"That man shouldn't have cheated!" she declared, throwing up her hands. "I was winning fairly and he was looking at the banker's cards before they were thrown."

He caught her upper arms in both hands and dragged her forward. She toppled off the seat and against his chest, flattening her hand against the warm plane of muscle there. Her heart was pounding, certainly he had to feel it, just as she felt his even through all the layers of propriety that separated them.

"This isn't a fucking card match with your spinster friends, Marianne. *That man* was coming for you. Likely no one at that table would have stopped him from hitting you or worse. It *isn't* a game there."

She bit her lip and tried not to think of the loud anger of the man she had accused. Of the fear that had blossomed in her chest when he lunged for her. The relief when Sebastian had appeared like some knight in a children's story and ridden to her rescue.

She stared up at him, his blue eyes almost gray in the darkness. His fingers loosened on her arms slightly and one lifted to brush her hair away from her cheek.

"I wouldn't have forgiven myself if I hadn't gotten there in time," he whispered.

She blinked at that admission, softly but powerfully made. "I'll—I'll be more careful next time."

The carriage slowed to a stop and he released her, letting her go back to her seat. "Next time," he repeated, and his expression grew shocked. "You mean you intend to go back to that place?"

"Or something like it. I can't promise I won't," she said, stepping down without waiting for the driver to help her. She certainly didn't need the humiliation of more prying eyes.

Sebastian followed at her heels. "Do you hear how mad that sounds?"

"No!" she said as she walked into the house. She dropped her voice and made for the stairs in the hopes he wouldn't follow her, though of course he did. "Sebastian, I *will* be careful. But I rather enjoyed the atmosphere until the game went awry. I'd like to see more of the hells. I've heard of one called the Donville Masquerade from the whispers of some of the married ladies and—"

He dragged her into her chamber, shutting the door behind her and spinning her to pin her against it. "You cannot go there!" he said. "Not there."

"Sebastian," she said, pushing against his chest. This time he didn't let her go but held her there.

"Goddamn it, Marianne. You may try to be more, but you're still so innocent," he said. "And if you push too hard you might get hurt. And not just by a misplaced fist. I never want that for you."

"You are just like my brother," she said, shoving him harder and making him step aside where he dragged a hand through his hair in clear frustration. "You want *nothing* for me. You made it more than clear. But you have no hold over me, Sebastian. You don't get to decide what I do."

"You think you know what I want when it comes to you?" He stepped toward her and suddenly he felt so big in the little room she'd had to herself her entire life. He felt like he stole the air, stole the heat, stole everything. "I don't want *nothing* for you, Marianne. In fact, I fear I want too much."

He was moving closer and closer, his gaze holding her so steady that she felt pinned in place. When he reached her he caught her arms yet again, but this time there was no desperation, no force, there was just…passion. All of it increased when he tugged her against his chest once more and kissed her.

She should have refused him. After all, it was less than a week before that he had declared they couldn't do this because of his loyalty to her brother. She had vowed never to pursue him again, no matter how much it ached to do so.

But she couldn't pull away. He was a magnet and she was held to him by forces of nature. As his tongue drove against hers, she lifted against him, grasping at his lapels the way he'd grabbed Lanford's, trying to mold herself close enough that he couldn't separate them.

She was trembling as his kiss deepened and then slowed. The passion didn't cool, but it became more metered as his hands stole away from her arms and down her back, across her hips, around her backside where he lifted her against him with a deep, rumbling groan of what she recognized was desire. And her own body answered, thrumming with the same, aching in a way she understood now that he had touched her.

She didn't want it to end. She didn't want him to pull away

again. Not tonight. Not now when she was so close to a taste of something she had longed for even when it had no name.

"Marianne," he moaned against her mouth, then he kissed her again, relentless and desperate.

"Please," she murmured, clinging tighter to him. "Please don't push me away. Please don't."

He pulled back a fraction, their lips still almost touching, and looked at her through a hooded gaze. "You know what you're asking."

"Yes," she whispered. "Better than anyone. But what is there to save myself for, Sebastian? The kind of man who would, as you said, abandon me to be attacked while he flirted with someone else? For the wall of every ballroom until I'm too old for invitations unless I'm serving as the chaperone for a niece? In this, I think *you* are the innocent, for you have no idea what it is like to be so certain that your future will be empty. At least let me have this."

He dropped his forehead to her shoulder with a shaky breath even as his hands continued to stroke the length of her body. Then he lifted his head and slid a hand into her hair to tilt her face up toward him.

"If you change your mind, you only have to say no," he said softly before his mouth returned to hers with more heat, more power and more purpose than before. And as she swirled into the dark heat of his desire, she knew that everything in her life was about to change and she couldn't wait.

CHAPTER 15

S ebastian had always considered himself a man in control. He
made wise choices when it came to his sexual quarry and he
never put himself in a position where he couldn't escape. But
tonight, as he backed Marianne across the antechamber and into
her bedroom on trembling legs, he couldn't say no. Even though he
should. Even though he would ruin her, ruin himself by what he
was about to do.

He needed her more than breath right now. When he thought of
some brute towering over her, fist raised in violence, he needed to
ease the horror of that image by making her lift in pleasure, not
duck in fear.

He pushed all those thoughts aside and gently parted his mouth
from hers. He turned her back to him and began to unfasten the
long line of buttons along the back of her pretty gown. She shivered
as his fingers stroked the soft skin he revealed and blushed as he
parted the dress wide before he let her face him again.

"Do you know how much I wanted to see you that night in the
orangery?" he asked as he slipped a finger beneath the edge of her
gown and began to tug, drawing the satin fabric over her shoulder,
down her upper arm, repeating the action on the other side before

he let the dress fold forward and reveal the pretty chemise beneath.

"You did?" she murmured, her voice shaking like her body shook. Fear and anticipation in one. He wanted to make it only pleasure that made her tremble.

He nodded. "All I could think about was you, touching you, seeing you, tasting you. Tonight I want to do all those things."

Perhaps if he did, it would burn this need for her away, lost in the fire he was stoking in them both. It had to, didn't it? Make this drive stop? At least he had to try.

She stared at him a long moment, long enough that he feared she might have become overwhelmed and want to say that one little word that would bring this to an end. Even though that would be better for them both, he found himself praying to every deity he'd ever heard of that she wouldn't.

But at last she pressed her palms against her hips and tugged her gown down to drop around her feet.

"Yes," she whispered.

He caught his breath at the sight of her in only her chemise and stockings, standing in firelight, so beautiful he could hardly stand it. Why had he not realized how beautiful she was before? Why had no other man every written soliloquies about her exquisiteness? Plucked her like some rare rose to decorate hallowed halls? They were all fools, him included.

"Am I a disappointment?" she asked, her hands coming forward to clench against her stomach.

He shook his head. "Far from it. I am drinking you in, savoring every moment of the gift of seeing you like this."

"You're the only man who ever has," she said. "I know you know that, but I admit it makes me nervous."

"Excited?" he asked as he moved forward and slipped a finger beneath the thin chemise strap, lowering it gently.

She nodded again and then inhaled sharply when he drew her hand through the chemise strap and revealed one gorgeous breast.

He cupped her, measuring her weight, stroking a thumb over her distended nipple as she dipped her head back and let out a shaky sigh of pleasure.

He couldn't resist the sleek expanse of her throat and brought his lips there, nibbling and kissing the column until her hands came up into his hair and she leaned into him for support.

"Tell me what it will be like," she whispered.

He lifted his head from her neck and met her gaze, holding there as he removed the other strap of her chemise and tugged it away so she was naked for him. He drank in the curves of her, the softness, the undeniable draw.

"I'll put you on the bed," he said, hearing how breathless he sounded. "And I'm going to make you ready for me. I'm going to explore every inch of your body until you are writhing, clamping a hand over your mouth so no one in this house hears you moaning my name."

She swallowed hard and her pupils dilated. He smiled at the reaction, at how responsive she was.

"Eventually I won't be able to hold back anymore. And I'll need to be inside of you. I'll start with my fingers. I'll feel how slick you are with desire as I ready you. It will drive me mad, it will make me ache to feel you pulse around me."

"Sebastian," she whimpered.

He chuckled as he backed her toward the bed. "I'll undress—"

"Will I get to touch you then?" she asked.

"Fuck," he muttered, and his hands shook as he pressed her back to the edge of the high mattress, letting his fingers stroke over her bare skin.

She was only in her stockings now and she looked good enough to devour. He would have to be very careful not to go too fast, but when she said things like that, when she made him picture her mouth and hands on him, it broke some of the thin threads that made up the rope of his control.

"Yes, you'll touch me. But it won't be to ready me, Marianne, because I've been hard for you for days, weeks." He caught her hips as he kissed her again, drinking deeply of her taste and the way she surrendered and arched against him. He pulled away and lifted her so she was on the edge of the bed, their faces more even now.

"Your legs will be wide for me, like they were that wonderful night in the orangery," he continued while he cupped both breasts and massaged them. She whimpered and he continued, loving how she shifted against him. "And you'll be dripping so when I finally rub my cock against you, it will feel so good for both of us. I'll slide inside, very gently this time."

"It will hurt?" she gasped.

He heard both her desire and the touch of fear in her tone. Of course she would be fearful, ladies were often told that this act would not be pleasant. And some men, he would not call them gentlemen, made no attempt to help it be so.

He lowered his mouth to one nipple and began to stroke his tongue across it. He sucked and she turned her mouth into her shoulder to stifle a little cry. How he wished they were at his house instead of her brother's so he could hear her moan and gasp and cry out at full voice. Like it was an opera of pleasure.

"It might a little, since you're untried. But if I've done my duty, you'll be very wet to ease the way. I'll be gentle, even though you'll be driving me so mad by then that I'll want to claim you like a wild animal."

Her gaze jerked to his and he could see how she liked that descriptor. The idea of him losing control and pounding into her, rough and desperate. It was too bad this could only be one very imprudent night, for he'd love to get to the point where he could learn all her likes. Teach her how to unleash her wild. Teach her how to tame his.

He swallowed at that unwanted thought. He'd avoided being tamed for a very long time. He didn't want that.

"And then what?" she asked, smoothing her hands over his still fully clothed shoulders and chest.

"I thrust into you, over and over. I rotate my hips against you so that you feel the echo of me in your clitoris. And you start to rise in a rhythm no dance master ever taught you but you'll know by heart. You'll feel the pleasure bloom between your legs, like it did the night I licked you. And you'll come and it will ripple around me and drive me to the edge."

She was trembling and she nodded. "What happens when you reach the edge?"

"I come. Different from you. I won't spend inside of you, so we won't create a child. But it will be glorious. It will rock the world from its axis for a few brilliant moments."

"Sebastian?" she whispered.

He nodded and met those dark brown eyes, losing himself for a moment in the warmth of them. "Yes?"

"I'm so wet already," she whispered. "I can feel it on my thighs."

He felt his eyes widen at that unexpected, wicked sentence. Goddamn, but this woman had depths she hid. She was a natural at eroticism and it drove him wild.

"Can you now," he drawled, pleased he could still utter a sentence when she was saying such things.

"So if you want to skip the first part…"

He laughed as she trailed off and then lowered her back on the bed with her legs hanging off the side. "Oh sweet, the first part is so wonderful. I wouldn't want to skip a thing."

And he realized it was true. He didn't want to miss a moment of this wicked, stolen night with her. He wanted to savor each one just as he savored her body. He knew that he wouldn't come out of this unchanged, any more than she would. But for the first time in his life, that thought didn't worry him. It excited him. As did she as he lowered his mouth back to her throat and began a lazy trail down the apex of her body.

She was his tonight. He wasn't going to rush anything.

∽

S ebastian's mouth was hot on her bare skin as he trailed it along her collarbone and then between her breasts. Marianne tried to stay in the moment as he paused there and kissed a heated trail to the breast he hadn't kissed or sucked earlier. She hadn't known that her body was such an instrument, one that could be played by the right man. That was him, for every time he stroked his fingers over her skin, every time he licked or sucked her, it was like he brought some new part of her to life.

She rose up against his tongue, digging her hands into his thick hair as he sucked her nipple gently, then harder, and sent sparks careening through every nerve of her body. How had she never known she could feel this kind of pleasure? Or was it only accessible with this man, who was so much more experienced than she was? Who knew how to wake her like she was some fairytale princess in a distant tower.

He returned to the other breast, taking his time to tease and torment. What she had said to him earlier, the words that had made his eyes widen and his hands grip tighter at her body, was true. She already felt so wet. If that was what he needed to take her, he had it in spades.

And yet he didn't rush. His mouth glided lower, across her ribcage, along her belly as he smoothed his hands to her hips. She expected him to duck between her legs like he had before, but instead he nibbled the line of her hip and down her outer thigh. She was writhing by then, covering her mouth just as he'd said she would to keep the moans and gasps of pleasure from being too loud.

He looked up at her with a wicked, knowing smile as he dragged his mouth across the line where her stockings were tied to her thighs. He caught one end of the bow in his teeth and drew back, unknotting the ribbon and loosening the stocking. She sat up on her elbows, unable to stop staring at him with her clothing between his teeth, his hands denting her flesh, his eyes flashing with heated desire.

She had never imagined she could make a man look like that. Most especially not this man. This known lover of women much more interesting than she.

He dropped the ribbon from his teeth and ducked his head to kiss her thigh again. "God, you drive me mad."

He moved to the other thigh and untied that ribbon as well. Then he began to roll her stockings down, tracing the flesh he revealed with his tongue. He licked down her thigh, over her knee and across her calf. He nipped her ankle gently and she gasped at unexpected pleasure.

When he tossed the stocking over his shoulder, he cupped her opposite leg with both hands and glided back up the length of her until he could repeat the motion.

And now she was fully naked, splayed out on her bed, nothing to hide her or protect her. She was afraid, but not as much as she could be. Mostly she was excited, trembling with sensation, ready for him to cover her and let her feel his weight.

But he didn't. When he reached her thigh with his tongue, this time he edged higher, opening her wider with his shoulders. "Sebastian," she gasped, gripping his still-clothed shoulders as he licked her sex.

"Oh yes, say my name, Marianne. Say it over and over while you quake," he grunted, and spread her open wider with his thumbs.

He dove into her sex, swirling his tongue across her, sucking her, doing all those wicked things she'd dreamed of since that night in the orangery. She lifted into him, clenching the edge of the bed with one hand while she tugged at his hair with the other. And all the while she moaned his name, her voice broken as he lifted her to the very highest peak of pleasure.

But he didn't let her fall. Not like last time. He simply tortured, keeping her on the edge with expert precision. Only when she was trembling and bracing and reaching for pleasure did he pull away, his mouth slick with her juices, and rose to his full height.

Without breaking eye contact with her, he stripped out of his clothing at what could only be described as lightning speed. His jacket joined her dress on the floor, then his waistcoat. When he finally tugged the linen shirt over his head she gasped.

He was so stunningly beautiful. Like a statue in the museum, all angles and muscle. But he was alive. He was warm and moving, hers to touch, if only for this night.

He removed his boots with a strangled curse at the effort and then his trousers and there was his cock. That instrument of pain to some and pleasure to many. She had never seen one of those. All those statues she'd compared him to already had them covered or broken off in an attempt to force modesty. His was hard and jutted up against his stomach.

"I understand what the fuss is about," she murmured as he returned to her with a wide smile.

"So many compliments," he whispered. She reached for him, gripping his base, stroking to the head. He bent his head back over his shoulders and barked out, "Marianne!"

"Was that wrong or right?" she asked, hesitating.

"Very right," he gasped. "Do it again."

She stroked again and he looked into her eyes as he moaned. Just as when he'd touched her, she felt the tingle that answered. Pleasuring him was just as much a pleasure to her. But she wanted more than this.

She wanted the other things he'd described in such detail. She wanted to feel him inside of her, she wanted to be claimed at last.

"Please," she whispered as she rested back on the bed.

He shook his head. "You dangling off the side is very nice when I eat your pretty pussy, but when I take you, you won't be half off your bed. Onto the pillows, please."

She scooted back and he crawled up with her, covering her at last. She expected him to take instantly, but he made no move to do so. He pushed her hair, which had come out of its style as they kissed and teased, out of her face and then leaned down to kiss her so very gently that it brought tears to her eyes.

She tasted herself on his lips, arousing and also proof that he was taking care of her. And she loved him for it. She'd felt that in the orangery, but it was more powerful now. More overwhelming and bigger.

She opened her eyes and looked up at him as he shifted to stroke his cock against her as promised. It felt so good that she whimpered.

In that moment he began to push into her body. The emotions mixed with the sensation of the invasion and she gasped as she lifted up into him, taking him farther inside. There was no pain, more a slight discomfort at being filled. But when he bent his head to kiss her again and held still inside of her, the discomfort faded. She was left only with the tingling power of being joined with this man she loved.

The echo of that truth kept ricocheting, meeting with his first full thrust and drawing her pleasure higher instantly. She gripped his bare shoulders, burying her face into his flesh and crying out in a muffled tone. He took again, rotating his hips to hers. She followed suit and the pleasure ticked higher again.

Over and over he took, each thrust drawing her back to the edge. Each mounting feeling making her heart swell even more. *This* was the man she loved and he was doing this wonderful thing with her. This thing no one could take away. She felt the ripple of pleasure, increasing every time he moved, and then it turned to a torrent as wave after wave of release washed over her.

He thrust through it, a little faster now, a little harder, his hands tugging her closer, like they could merge in this moment of searing sensation. She almost believed they could, she certainly wished it were true.

His neck tensed, cords of tendons outlined on the flesh, and then he withdrew and stroked his cock. She leaned up again, watching as he came. It was different than when she did, for thick ropes of fluid came from the head of him, splashing hot on her stomach and thighs as he moaned low and hungry.

He collapsed down over her again, his arms coming around her, his mouth finding hers as their panting breaths merged and quieted together at last and this moment, the one he claimed they were stealing, washed over her. She knew three things as the warmth and comfort filled her: she was in love and she never wanted this to end.

But she also knew that it would. That was the thing she knew most. It would end. Because whatever she felt, Sebastian didn't. And she had to keep herself from being too tied up in wanting him to return those feelings or else she would end up with a broken heart.

CHAPTER 16

Sebastian had never been one to lounge in bed with a lover, and yet the idea of letting Marianne go and departing her room felt unbearable. She was curled so beautifully into his side, so warm and perfect in his arms. He wanted to sleep here next to her. He wanted to wake up in a few hours and roll over to pleasure her all over again.

He stared at her ceiling, the plaster swirled into the shapes of stars, and tried to meter both his breathing and these odd thoughts.

She clenched a fist against his bare chest and he felt her look at him. When he forced himself to do the same, he found her expression relaxed and sated and she smiled at him as if everything they'd done was perfectly right.

It most definitely wasn't.

"I never imagined," she whispered, her fingers now tracing little patterns on his chest that somehow lit his body on fire all over again.

"So you don't regret it?" he asked as he caught the hand that was so arousing him and lifted it to kiss her knuckles gently.

She sat up and turned toward him. "Never," she said with feeling. "And I want you to understand something, Sebastian."

He drew a shaky breath. "What is that?"

"I have *no* expectations because of this. As you said, it was a night stolen in time, a gift for me, and I hope not too much of a chore for you."

His eyes widened. "Do you think that was a *chore*?" He shook his head. "Great Lord, Marianne, I haven't had to practice so much control in years so I wouldn't come five seconds after entering a woman. I promise you, that was only a pleasure for me."

He had said the words and they were true, but they felt entirely vulnerable. Still, when she smiled he didn't particularly care. He didn't want her to think so low of herself, he didn't want her to believe he'd made love to her out of pity.

"Good. Then we both benefitted." She relaxed back on her pillows with a satisfied sigh. He rolled to his side and watched her for a moment, memorizing how she looked when she was still lazy and content with orgasm.

"*This* is what I meant when I said to you that I was no gentleman," he said slowly.

She glanced at him with a blush. "Because I was untouched."

He nodded. "I've taken something that many men value greatly. And I've damaged your standing on the marriage mart."

She laughed, but there was something hollow to it. "Sebastian, I haven't had standing on the marriage mart in years. There is nothing to damage." She sighed. "After Claudia's death, I realized the value in *living*. Not just existing from wall to wall at endless boring balls, but *living*."

He frowned as he thought of the list he'd discovered earlier. The one that was still lying on the dressing table across the room. She didn't know he'd found it. For now, he intended to keep it that way. But that didn't mean he couldn't probe a little with that new knowledge.

"I suppose it must have felt like Claudia left things undone before her sudden death," he said carefully.

Her breath became a little shallower, a little shakier. "Yes. I know she felt that way. You wouldn't understand, as you've always been so golden, but for an unmarried lady, especially one who is so firmly on the shelf as Claudia was or I am, life often feels like a waiting game. We aren't allowed to be...to be *too much*. To be truly free. We're expected to wait quietly and politely for a husband to arrive. Perhaps after we gift him with an heir and a spare we'll be granted some ability to try new things, but it's all within reason and only with permission."

He had never considered that. His own life was nothing but freedom. Perhaps too much, considering he'd just ruined his best friend's maiden sister. His own friend.

"That must be frustrating," he said softly, taking her hand and folding her fingers in between his gently.

She shivered. "Yes."

"And is that why you've been so much more...daring as of late?"

"I suppose there's no hiding from you now, is there?" she said with a little laugh. "You've seen me naked."

"I've very much enjoyed that," he teased so that her mood would lighten.

"Because you are a rake," she teased back. Then her laughter faded. "But yes. I suppose I do feel obligated to live a little more now. For her. But also for me."

He nodded. "That I *do* understand," he said, and stared up at her ceiling again. "Living someone else's life."

"Do you?" she asked.

He let out his breath slowly as his mind turned to thoughts. Dark thoughts. Painful thoughts he often pushed away. But perhaps if he shared them that would make him even more of her ally in this quest of hers to complete her friend's list. At least he could protect her if she did.

But would he be able to protect himself if he spoke of the painful memories that wracked him? Would he give too much of himself and never be able to get that portion back from her?

"Sebastian?" she said softly, and her fingers traced his jawline with such gentleness that he couldn't help but close his eyes and lean into the pressure of her hand. It was soothing somehow. Healing.

"Did you know I had a younger brother?"

He heard her breath catch and turned his head to look at her. She shook her head. "No."

"George," he said, and then corrected himself. "Georgie, I called him. He was two years younger. My mother and father despised each other down to their very cores, and as soon as the earl had his heir and spare my mother separated herself from us. She went to London, lived her own life, and I doubt had even a thought for us."

Marianne winced. "I had no idea."

"Yes, I make it so that no one does," he said softly, watching the firelight play off her face. "I'm very careful to do so."

Understanding dawned over her face and her hand came to rest on his bare chest again. "Were you close to your brother?"

"Oh yes. You know how our father was, so mean tempered and cruel. He had no interest in either of us, really, and left us to be raised by servants and the woods around the estate. And Georgie and I loved to run and race and play." He could picture his brother now, dark blond hair so like Sebastian's own being ruffled in the wind, little pudgy legs working so hard to keep up with his older brother. Sebastian had always tried to slow himself down so George wouldn't get lost.

His eyes stung at the memory and he blinked away the sensation so he could continue, "When he was six and I was eight, we were playing out at the little lake on the country estate. We'd been trying to build a boat all summer and it was not going well. But we still valiantly tried to row it out. Then…"

He trailed off and squeezed his eyes shut as images bombarded him.

"Sebastian, it's all right," she said gently, and he realized he was breathing heavily. "I'm here."

He caught her hand and held it for a long moment, trying to

focus on the softness of her fingers in his. "We took on water," he whispered at last. "It started to sink. We were laughing at first but... but then his trouser leg got caught on one of the nails I hadn't fully pounded into the wood and he—he couldn't get loose. I couldn't get him loose. I kept diving down, I kept tugging him, but I wasn't strong enough and he—he—he—"

"He drowned," she said softly.

He sucked in a sharp, harsh breath at those two words. "Yes."

Suddenly her arms came around him, pulling him close. He rested his head on her shoulder, trying to get control of the emotions that pressed down on him, threatening to crush him. *This* was why he never spoke of that moment to anyone. It stole his control. It made him weak to feel these feelings all over again, like he was still at the lake, like he was still watching his brother die under the water.

"I almost drowned too," he said at last. "But I managed to get to shore. My father was so angry at me."

"Not grieved?" she whispered.

He shook his head. "He kept saying that I stole his spare. That I ruined the order of things. Otherwise he gave not a damn about his lost son. He made the servants go out to retrieve his body and forced me to watch from the shore as punishment while *he* went to some ball like nothing had happened."

"He went to a ball?"

His lips pursed with heated hatred. "He said that once the truth was out about the death, he wouldn't be allowed to attend anything while he moved through the prescribed mourning period. He didn't want to miss one last chance to carouse."

He felt a drop of water hit his shoulder and looked up to find that tears were streaming down Marianne's face. Tears for him. The ones he forced himself not to shed.

"Oh Sebastian, that is terrible. I'm so dreadfully sorry you and your brother were treated with such callous disregard. You didn't deserve that," she said, her fingers brushing over his face.

He froze. Didn't deserve that. No, he hadn't. Georgie hadn't. Sebastian had never allowed that fleeting thought to develop in his mind beyond a flutter, because when it did, the anger that followed was wild. He'd had to keep it in check during his childhood when he was too small to battle his cruel father.

And as an adult, he had always worked not to be like the man who raised him. He didn't want to be cruel. He chose flighty, he chose rakish, he chose anything but serious so that he wouldn't spiral into the depths he feared he wouldn't escape.

But her words reminded him of the desperate unfairness of his childhood. Of his loss and how alone he'd been in it.

"Were you allowed any time to grieve?" she asked gently.

"Of course not," he choked out. "I wore a black band for exactly the three months that Society expects, but I wasn't allowed to speak about Georgie to anyone, nor was anyone allowed to talk to me about him."

"That is dreadful. Monstrous!"

He shrugged even though there was nothing dismissive about how he felt over this topic. "I tell you this not to obtain your pity, but because I *do* understand the idea of living for another person."

"Yes, I can see how you would," she said. "And I can also understand even more deeply now why your relationship to Finn is so important to you."

"Yes, Finn." Sebastian rubbed a hand over his face and stared at the ceiling. He'd known exactly the consequences he might face by spending this night with Marianne. If Delacourt discovered it, there might be pistols at dawn, not just an end to their friendship.

"He met you in school," she said softly. "What were you both? Ten?"

"Yes," he said. "And immediately we were drawn to each other. I suppose with your own wretched parents, we must have recognized kindred spirits in that. We'd only been friends a few months when my mother died. I wasn't allowed to attend her services—my father's doing. And I...I admit I collapsed. Your brother held me up. That solidified our bond."

"He *became* your brother," she said.

"He did. He is."

They both were quiet for a moment, lost in thought in the quiet of the room. Then she leaned over and pressed a brief kiss to his lips before she slipped from the bed and began hunting around for her shift amongst their tangled clothing on the floor.

"I would never threaten that, you know," she said as she found the item and tugged it over her head, covering herself. "I would *never* do anything to take him from you. He won't find out about this. It will be our secret."

He stared at her, standing in the firelight, so beautiful with her hair tangled around her shoulders, in the flimsiest of fabrics. Her expression was only kindness and understanding, acceptance of the limitations he would force on this joining.

Why couldn't he feel the same acceptance? Why did her gentle release of him from obligation make him frustrated rather than relieved?

He pushed the troubling thoughts aside and got to his feet too. Once he had dressed in his trousers, he faced her. "You are too good, Marianne. Too sweet."

Her lips thinned as if that wasn't a compliment. Still, she shrugged. "I do try. Now will you help me dress?"

He wrinkled his brow. "Dress?"

"Yes. I'm going to fix myself and then call for my maid. I'll tell her I was reading late into the night and dozed off. She'll help me undress and it will be like any other night. She'll never know that it was, in fact, so magical and wondrous."

He nodded slowly. "That's very clever, not that I would expect less. Yes, I'll help you."

He did so, trying not to note every brush of his fingers as he fastened her dress, not to get lost as he watched her put her stockings on and tie the ribbons he'd loosened with his teeth as she writhed above him.

At last she was fixed and he dressed, too, feeling her watch him from the corner of her eye from time to time.

"You know," he said as he fastened his waistcoat and shrugged on his jacket. "If you want to try living some more, I'm happy to continue helping you."

She tilted her head. "Are you?"

He nodded and thought of her list. "You said you wanted to return to a hell. Please let me escort you if you insist on doing that. I'll keep you far safer that that twat Lanford did."

She shook her head. "Lanford. Do you think he'll spread the word of this night?"

"No. He'd be a fool to do so and risk your brother's wrath. But I'll talk to him again tomorrow and ensure it."

"You would do that to protect me?" she asked, staring up at him with those brown eyes soft and filled with emotions he didn't want to define for fear he'd melt back into her.

"Of course. And myself," he said, turning away as if all this was nothing. "Delacourt would be furious if he knew you snuck out and I didn't inform him."

He moved through the antechamber and to the door that led to the hallway and she followed him. There they both stopped and she smiled up at him. She was so beautiful in that moment that he almost forgot how to breathe as he stared at her. It set him on his heels, took him off center and he had to physically force himself to return.

"Thank you again, Sebastian. I'll never forget this night."

He cupped her cheek, stroking his thumb over the softness there and sighed. "No, I don't think I will either."

He leaned in and kissed her. It would be the last time he'd do this. It had to be. So he savored it. Savored how she leaned up into him, how she shivered as her hands gripped his forearms to steady herself. Savored her taste and the way her tongue traced his.

Then he stepped away because he had to. Walked away because he had to. And feared he had left something very important behind with her. Something he hadn't realized was so deep a part of himself. Something he had to forget as he made his way back to his own chamber and what he knew would be a long and sleepless night.

CHAPTER 17

The next morning, Marianne stared at her reflection in the mirror as Hannah stood behind her fixing her hair. She felt she ought to look different after her passionate night in Sebastian's arms, but somehow she was still just…her. He hadn't made her different, at least not where anyone could see.

She forced a smile at her maid. "I do want to apologize, Hannah, for waking you so late last night. I cannot believe I fell asleep fully dressed."

"Of course not, my lady! It's my duty, I'm pleased to do it." She pinned a few more locks of Marianne's hair into place and then said, "I didn't want to ask you last night, as I could see you were tired, but did Lord Ramsbury ever find you?"

Marianne tensed at the mention of the very man she'd been daydreaming about a moment before. "L-Lord Ramsbury? What do you mean? I haven't been out of my chamber today. Was he looking for me this morning?"

"Oh no, my lady. Not today. I meant last night."

Marianne shook her head. "I don't know what you're talking about."

"The earl found me in the hall as I was going back to servants' quarters after the gathering broke up. He asked where you were as he had looked for you in the library and didn't find you there in your usual spot. I said I thought you might have gone to read in your room. He did tell me that whatever he had to say to you could wait until tomorrow, but then I saw him going toward your chamber." Hannah stepped back to admire her handiwork. "There you are, my lady. And I must say you are positively glowing this morning. You really do look well in that blue."

"Thank you," Marianne said as an acknowledgment of the compliment, but her mind was racing. "Er, well, I'll look for him this morning and see if he still has something to discuss."

Her maid turned to go and after she had, Marianne leapt to her feet and began to pace the room. Why had Sebastian been looking for her last night after she'd snuck out to the hell with Lanford? And why hadn't he mentioned it after he'd found her there or in the time they'd spent together afterward?

"You're being silly," she assured herself as she moved across the room toward the bed where he had made love to her last night.

After all, just because he'd been seen coming toward her chamber didn't mean he'd actually gone there. He could have always intended to go to the hell, just as he'd told her last night, and speaking to her was only a quick stop on his way, easily forgotten when he thought she'd retired.

She frowned as she went to the dressing table by the window where she'd been sitting earlier. After Sebastian had gone last night, before she'd called for Hannah, she'd realized she left Claudia's list out in her haste to go to the hell. It had been left unfolded on the table before her, there for anyone to find, along with the notes she'd made about her progress.

Was it possible Sebastian *had* come into this room and actually found the list? Read it? Seen her notes, including the one about going to a hell with Lanford and *that* was why he had pursued her there?

Her hands began to sweat and she rubbed them on her skirt as she tried to meter her breath. She was likely being ridiculous to think those things. But if she wasn't…if he *had* found the list…

The very idea made her heart throb faster and her hands shake. She didn't want anyone to know what she was doing, but Sebastian least of all. The time they'd spent together recently, including last night, had meant so much to her. She didn't want it to be marred by whatever his thoughts were about the list. About her crossing things off of it.

"There is only one way to know," she said to herself. "Go find him and ask."

She turned toward the door, but she couldn't seem to make herself move forward. She felt frozen in place, anxiety washing through her in long, echoing waves. Seeing Sebastian after last night was going to be difficult enough. She'd already been planning how to pretend like she didn't know his taste, the feel of his skin, his expression when he lost all control.

But if it turned out he knew her secret, that was going to be even worse.

Somehow she forced her feet to move and exited the chamber. Whatever would happen, would happen. And she had to be brave enough to face it, just as she was trying to be brave enough to finish Claudia's list. She owed it to herself to find out the truth.

Even if it changed everything between her and Sebastian all over again.

Sebastian entered the breakfast room at far earlier an hour than he would normally do so, especially after a late night making love to a beautiful woman. But his chamber and bed had brought no sleep, only restless tossing and turning as he relived every one of Marianne's sighs. Every gentle reaction to secrets he'd never intended to spill out like poison from a wound.

But all those thoughts were pushed away as he realized the only other guest in attendance so early was Charles Lanford. He was sitting at the table, coffee in one hand, a newspaper in the other, though he was paying no attention to either. He jolted as he saw Sebastian and struggled to his feet. "Good-good morning, my lord," he said.

Sebastian pursed his lips. He had things to discuss with this man, but he wasn't sure he was in the right frame of mind to do so. The idea that Lanford had left Marianne exposed the night before conjured up far more rage than was healthy for either of them. And it could certainly reveal too much if he spewed it out now.

"Lanford," he growled as he moved to the sideboard to look at the spread.

The idea of food had no interest to him, so he poured tea instead and then joined the other man at the table. When he sat, so did his companion and the two stared at each other for what felt like a tense lifetime.

"Lady Marianne was unharmed after—after the unfortunate incident last night?" Lanford asked at last.

"Yes," Sebastian said, trying not to think of her terrified face as the man she'd been playing cards with had swung toward her in potent, drunken rage. "No thanks to you. What the hell were you thinking, taking her there and then exposing her to danger when you left her side?"

Lanford shook his head. "When I asked her to join me, I was only thinking of us having a good time together. I've been to that hell before, it's usually fairly calm. Tame as far as those places go."

"Tame for men with experience, *not* a sheltered lady like Marianne," Sebastian ground out.

Lanford nodded. "Yes. You are right, of course. And I knew it was a bit inappropriate, but she seemed so excited about the idea. She lit up like a candle when we discussed it at the gathering. It was impossible to resist her when she was like that."

Sebastian tensed. He knew exactly what Lanford meant. There was something magical about Marianne when she became excited about a topic. Like she was ignited from within, like she glowed. Like she could pull a man into her joy and he'd never feel pain again. The fact that Lanford had seen any portion of that glorious part of her made Sebastian's chest hurt. He knew what that feeling was. He didn't like it.

"So she seduced you, poor innocent thing," he drawled, hoping his tone didn't reveal his darker emotions on that subject.

"No," Lanford rubbed a hand through his hair. "Of course not, no. I only…I…I hoped that escorting her might allow me to get a bit closer to the lady."

That ugly jealousy doubled in an instant and Sebastian's hands began to tingle. He shook them out at his sides. "You have an interest in Lady Marianne?"

"I-I did," Lanford admitted, his head bending as if he were almost ashamed. "I hadn't given her a thought until that night at the Brighthollow ball. But it was impossible not to once the room seemed to turn to her. I approached her there, and I actually found her to be charming. Ultimately, I began to think it would be a good match for us both. She would be removed from the shelf, after all. She must want that after she's been so long overlooked. How could she say no?"

Sebastian gripped his hands in front of him. "That is a romantic judgment of the lady."

"Oh, but I don't think I wouldn't benefit, as well." Lanford said. "I know I would move up in the world through her family connections. Her dowry."

Sebastian turned his head at that rote recitation of entirely normal, but infuriating reasons that a man would want Marianne. Not for her sweetness or her intelligence or her bravery, but for her associations, or more to the point, the associations of her powerful brother. That this man would think the mere act of removing her from the shelf would be something she ought to appreciate.

"I'm certain her brother would not be pleased at your method of courtship," Sebastian managed through clenched teeth. "At any rate, by the time I arrived and came to her aid you had abandoned her side to flirt with other ladies. How does that fit into your supposed desire to court her?"

Lanford shifted, his cheeks darkening to deeper red. "Well, when we were riding over to the hell in my carriage...she..."

There was something about the way Lanford was clenching his hands nervously and hemming and hawing that made Sebastian want to put a fist through his nose.

"What is it, man?" he snapped. "Spit it out."

"She only talked about...about you," Lanford finished.

Sebastian stared at him as the weight of each of those words hit him full in the chest. "I beg your pardon?"

"Any subject I brought up, she turned it toward you. When I asked about her brother's estate, she told me at least three tales of growing up there and spending time with you. When I inquired about her pursuits, she mentioned she was embroidering handker-chiefs for Christmas for *you* and for her brother." Lanford shook his head. "Even when I inquired about what she was currently reading, she said she was reading a gothic novel she borrowed from you because you thought she would enjoy it. She couldn't wait to speak to you about it when she was finished."

Sebastian felt like each word spoken was a dagger to his pounding heart. "I see," he managed to choke out. "So you don't like her friendship with me."

Lanford arched a brow and looked at Sebastian like he was a simpleton to put it in those terms. "Your friendship? I suppose I wouldn't like it if my potential wife was *friends* with such a known rake, no. But that isn't it. No, it was entirely clear, by the time we reached the hell, that Lady Marianne had no interest in my pursuit, not when her head was filled with thoughts of you. No matter how out of reach you are to a woman like her, she clearly considers you her ideal. I couldn't compete."

The room shifted around Sebastian and Lanford's words sounded like they were coming from under water. He was meant to respond now, though how to do so felt muddy with the knowledge he was being given.

The understanding it left him with.

"And so—" He cleared his suddenly thick throat. "And so you chose to abandon her to danger because it was clear she had no interest in you. How gentlemanly."

"I was distracted, I admit, and that was wrong." Lanford let out his breath in a long sigh. "I've no intention of ever spreading any stories, you know. Not about her. If that's your worry."

"I think it would be best if no one ever heard about what happened. For both your sakes. And mine, I suppose."

Lanford gave him an appraising look. "You're protective of her."

Sebastian pursed his lips. It should have been easy to brush off the statement. To dismiss it and her as meaningless beyond a long friendship. But he found he couldn't. The words wouldn't come anymore.

"I am," he finally said, and nothing else.

Lanford opened his mouth as if to say more, but before he could, Marianne strode into the breakfast room, hands clenched at her sides. "Sebastian, one of the maids said that you were—" She cut herself off and stopped short at the chamber door. "Oh, Mr. Lanford. I didn't...I didn't realize you were here."

Lanford and Sebastian both rose and Lanford gave a small bow. "Good morning, Lady Marianne. I am beyond pleased to see you unharmed after I was so remiss in my behavior last night."

She swallowed hard and looked from Lanford to Sebastian and back again. Sebastian could see she was nervous, her cheeks flushed as she brushed her palms along the skirt of her dress. He couldn't help but think of touching her thighs last night. Of the catch in her breath when he'd done so.

"I'm well, thank you for your concern," she said with a quick smile of comfort for the man. "If you've been torturing yourself about my experience, I free you from that worry. My evening was more than pleasant—" Her gaze darted to Sebastian again. "Aside from that one little nastiness at the card table." She stepped closer and extended a hand to Lanford. "May we still be friends, Mr. Lanford?"

Lanford hesitated but a moment before he came around the table to take her offered hand in both of his. There was an intimacy to that. Marianne held his gaze as he said, "Have I earned a continuing friendship with you, my lady, I'm greatly appreciative of that fact. Now I shall excuse myself and continue with my day, as it seems you had something to discuss with Lord Ramsbury."

He released Marianne and went to the chamber door where he cast one last glance toward Sebastian and then left the room. Left Sebastian alone with her.

"Good morning," he said softly.

Her cheeks darkened further. "Good morning."

"You look lovely."

She worried her hands in front of her. "I kept stealing glances at myself while Hannah was readying me and expected to look different...after."

"You do look different," he said as he moved to the sideboard. "May I get you tea?"

"No, thank you." She tilted her head. "How do I look different?"

He turned and leaned on the edge of the wooden table, allowing himself to drink in the look of her at his leisure. "You glow."

"Funny, that's what Hannah said, as well." She covered her now pink cheeks with both hands and he smiled despite his tangled thoughts and feelings about everything that had transpired in the last twenty-four hours.

"Well, I swear the reason why will remain a secret between us," he said. "On the subject of secrets, it seems Mr. Lanford will also keep his. He has no intention of speaking to anyone about your misadventures in the hell last night."

"Good." He could see her relax with that statement. "Very good. There's no reason for what happened to become common knowledge. It wouldn't reflect well on any party."

"No," he agreed, and stepped toward her. How he wanted to take her hand as Lanford had. Only if he did, he feared he would duck his head and kiss her. And then he'd want to do more than kiss her. Right here in the damned breakfast room. He cleared his throat.

"Were you looking for me for some other reason?" he asked.

She nodded and her expression changed, became more guarded. He found he didn't like even that small wall coming down between them, despite it being for the best. "Yes. Er, Hannah said you were trying to find me last night."

He swallowed. He'd all but forgotten that he had encountered Marianne's maid in the hall. Of course she would report back his actions to her. Ones he had lied about the previous night because he didn't want her to know he'd found her list.

"I was," he said carefully. "After the party broke up, I wanted to talk to you about Lanford."

"About Lanford?" she asked, her brow wrinkling. "Why would you wish to speak to me about him?"

"He's interested in you," he said, trying to keep his tone as mild as possible. "I guessed it yesterday—he confirmed it during our conversation this morning."

She sucked in a breath and her spine straightened. What felt like a dozen emotions passed over her countenance in that moment: surprise and disbelief, confusion and dismay. But two stood out the most to him. She appeared angry and she appeared interested.

"I thought you were only going to make sure that Mr. Lanford didn't discuss last night's unfortunate situation, not break bread with him and talk about something so private."

"His interest in you is *private*, is it?"

She shrugged. "Why wouldn't it be?"

"Considering what you and I did last night?" he asked.

Her eyes widened. "One has nothing to do with the other. How did that subject come up? Please tell me you weren't trying to barter away your pathetic friend to some other man, out of some fear I'll ask you for more than you've given."

"Of course not," he said, pushing off the sideboard and crossing toward her. "That wasn't it at all. But I can't believe you aren't dismissing his interest out of hand. *Charles Lanford?*"

She pursed her lips. "Should I dismiss it because I am so beneath him or he beneath me?"

Sebastian shook his head. This was coming out all wrong and he hated it. Hated that she was now staring at him with arms folded like a shield. Hated that she hadn't laughed off the attentions of some other man, even if Sebastian had done nothing to earn that. Hated that he could feel her anger directed at him with the same intensity with which she had bathed him in her passion the night before.

"You are certainly not beneath him," he said.

"Some would beg to differ. I am a spinster many seasons on the shelf. Yes, I have money and connection, but that's tempted no one in all the years I've been out. Do I need to remind you of my disastrous debut?"

"No."

She shook her head. "No, let me. Because you think you understand but you don't. My mother's death kept me from coming out for half a season, but that's not why I was shunned. She had a breakdown before her death."

"I know that, Marianne," he said, stepping toward her, hand outreached so that he could comfort her.

To his surprise she backed away. "No, you don't. *No one* knows. No one knows what I saw, what I endured. Not even my brother."

"Then tell me," he whispered, wanting to know her at such a deep place that he hadn't even realized it existed. "I hope you can trust me as much as I trusted you with a past kept in the shadows for far too long."

She shut her eyes and drew a shaky breath. Her pain was so clear, so powerful that it felt like a knife across this throat. "My mother...it was an arranged marriage like so many others. But she loved him. Or...perhaps it wasn't love at all. She tended to become obsessed with things, people, entirely focused on every part of them, needing them to be as tied to her. There was no one she felt that way about more than my father."

Sebastian flinched. "Not a good pick, I fear. I know he wasn't a kind man."

"No. And he loved to bounce her around on his wicked string. It was a game to him. It broke her down over the years. Just before my coming out, she discovered he had been living in one of his homes out in the countryside with his mistress while he kept her away in London. He'd never been so bold. She became…frenetic in a way I'd never seen. She wrote letters, three or four a day. I saw a few of them before she sent them. They were almost nonsensical and begged him to return, begged and begged."

"Did he answer?" he asked.

She shook her head. "Never once. After ten days like that, she just…stopped eating and drinking. At first I thought it was best to leave her to her own devices, let her calm herself. But she didn't. Then I began to insist she take care of herself, tried to tempt her and help her. Only she became angry. She went out of control. I'd never seen her like that. She destroyed her own chamber, she slammed herself into furniture and she—" Marianne cut herself off and swallowed hard. "She lashed out at the servants and at me, physically."

"She struck you?" he breathed.

Tears sparkled in her eyes as Marianne nodded slowly. "I'd been trying to keep the worst from Finn, but I *had* to reach out to him then. He had just purchased that old house of his on St. James, so he'd been distracted. He rushed over at once when I sent for him, saw what was happening. We kept trying to calm her, sent for doctors, they even tried to force feed her, but to no avail. She withered. Withered away as if the possibility of that man's love was all her sustenance. And she died of a broken heart."

Sebastian's own heart broke for Marianne and he took her hand.

She let him for a moment, clung to him like he could keep her upright. "Finn never told me," he breathed.

"He didn't know the part where she hit me, I knew it would only crush him more than he was crushed seeing her like that," she whispered. "I've carried that lonely burden every day since."

"I'm sorry I didn't know how terrible it was."

"It was even more terrible when the servants, who were loyal to my father after all, talked. The whispers of suicide and madness leaked out, even muted from the horrible reality. It was such a story, nothing the *ton* could possibly ignore. The wife of an earl in full collapse? That was just too good not to spread to every corner of Society. When I returned to the marriage mart after my mourning period, I was given side glances instead of being appraised for my potential as a match. Even when they forgot the foggy details, the damage was done. They might not recall fully why, but they know I'm not worth the time to pursue."

She had her chin lifted in strength but he could see the pain in her eyes. The heartbreak she had experienced and hidden. "Marianne," he whispered.

She pulled her hand away and kept on. "So if a gentleman of a certain quality and a reasonable handsomeness has *finally* expressed an interest in me, I'd be a fool not to at least consider his offer."

Sebastian's mouth dropped open. "You cannot mean that, Marianne."

She moved toward him now and her eyebrows knitted together. How many times had he watched her make that expression over the years. A little indication of her frustration. Again, he didn't like it directed at him. "Why would you care so much, Sebastian? You've made it clear that you cannot pursue a future with me even if you wished to, which you *don't*, because of your friendship with Finn."

He shook his head, trying to find an answer to her perfectly legitimate question. Why *did* he care? No, he wouldn't have chosen Lanford for her, even before the other man had exhibited such a lack of care for her. But certainly she had a right to have an interest in another man. In a life with someone who would grant her the chance to have more experiences. To have more freedoms. To have children and an increased standing with her peers.

Only he couldn't think of *anyone* he'd want to see in that role. The very idea of her arching her back beneath another man like she'd arched it beneath him, of her laughing with some other man at a breakfast table, of bringing her joys and excitements to him…it was an anathema.

He cleared his throat and forced the next words from his lips. "I suppose if you find yourself interested in Mr. Lanford, you are right that I shouldn't object. It isn't my place."

Her expression flickered with pain for a brief moment and then it was gone. "No. It isn't. Please excuse me, Sebastian, I think I forgot something in my chamber."

She pivoted then and walked from the room before he could respond. He turned away and pressed his hands onto the table before him, his breath coming short and harsh in the quiet of the room.

This wasn't how he'd wanted to interact with Marianne the morning after they made love. How he *had* wished to do so had been a foggy thing, but not this. Not facing her with tension, and not of the pleasant kind. Not her declaring that he should walk away and not take interest in the potential courtship of another man when her moans of his name still echoed in his ears.

"Fuck," he grunted.

"That isn't a good way to start the day," came a laughing voice behind him.

He turned to find Delacourt entering the room, and for a moment he tensed. But the smile on his friend's face seemed to indicate he'd heard nothing of Sebastian's exchange with Marianne. In fact, Delacourt looked lighter than he had in weeks before in London and Sebastian should have embraced that positive change. Instead, he had to force a smile.

"I don't suppose you have a suggestion on a better way then?" he asked.

"Some of the boys are going for a ride this morning. We'll do a bit of shooting before supper and the ball tonight. I've even arranged for a spread by the lake for tea."

Sebastian glanced toward the chamber door, as if he could call Marianne back to him if he concentrated hard enough. But then he nodded. "The air and companionship will do me good," he said. "But we must be sure to invite Mr. Lanford, as well."

Delacourt wrinkled his brow. "I wasn't aware you were so friendly with the man. I thought you didn't much care for him."

"Perhaps he'll grow on me."

"Very well, I'll be sure to have a personal invitation given to the man before I begin to ready myself for the outing. We depart in an hour."

Delacourt slapped Sebastian's bicep before he grabbed a pastry from the sideboard and exited the breakfast room. Sebastian sighed and moved to the window where he looked out at the garden behind the house. He jolted as he watched Marianne appear from the direction of the terrace stairs and walk through the bushes and plants.

It was good he'd have time away from her on this outing. Surely it would cool any residual feelings their night together had falsely created. And with Lanford within his sightline, he would also insure that Marianne didn't do anything foolish in her anger, either.

By the time of the ball that night, everything would be normal again. It had to be. There was no alternative.

CHAPTER 18

There had been many parties held at Garringford Corners over the years since her father's death when it had only been Marianne and Finn. During those parties her brother and his cronies often spent a day away participating in what Finn teased were "manly pursuits". In theory, she was invited to join in because Finn would never truly leave her out, but she'd more often than not welcomed the solitude, preparing for whatever events were next on the docket or reading and relaxing.

But today she had found herself watching the clock all afternoon. Listening for the footfalls of the gentleman. Of Sebastian in particular.

Now she sat in her chamber, fully dressed for supper and the ball which would follow, and she let her gaze move to the drawer in her dressing table where she had stashed Claudia's list earlier.

She hadn't yet looked at it since her night with Sebastian. Even with all the time alone, she almost hadn't *wanted* to look at it. To think about what she now had to cross off. Somehow doing so had a finality now that had never existed in the past.

Slowly, she pulled the list out and arranged her quill and ink on the dressing table before her. She scanned the paper, which now had so many items crossed off and careful notes in the margins.

She dipped her quill and slowly ran through the item in Claudia's hand that read *Play Faro in a Hell*. What her friend would have thought, seeing her there with a pile of winnings before her and later with an angry patron on the attack. Claudia had always been shy with strangers, almost painfully so. It was a triumph to be one of the few who saw her true bubbly personality and Marianne hoped Claudia would have cheered her on in her momentary victory.

"Thanks to all the games with you, dearest," she whispered to the list and the woman who had written it.

Then she scanned lower and her breath caught. One of the last items on the long inventory was *Have a Love Affair*. She stared at those words, written almost accusingly now that she was trying to determine if she should check them off.

A love affair implied some matter of time shared between two people. More than one encounter, something with more formality, even if everything was done in secret. Yet Sebastian made clear with his words and his deeds that last night was the one and only time they would share such a powerful act. So an affair? It didn't feel like that was the right word.

She sighed and used her pen to edit the list. *Take a Lover*, she wrote to the side and then slowly crossed off the item before she waved the paper in the air to dry the ink. Taking a lover would have to do, since she had no intention of pursuing another man for something with so much more depth like an affair.

She got to her feet, checking herself in the mirror once more before she made her way to the foyer where she and Finn would greet their arriving guests for tonight's festivities. She smiled at her reflection. Thanks to Hannah's handiwork, no longer did Marianne see a matronly spinster when she looked at her reflection. She might be no great temptation to any man, but she was no longer ill-suited for her own clothing. That was a triumph of some kind, she supposed.

She stepped into the hall and made her way to the stairs where she met with Mr. Lanford coming from the guest wing of the house.

"Ah, Lady Marianne," he said as he reached her. His gaze flitted over her and he smiled. "You do look a vision."

Heat rose to her cheeks at that compliment that felt truly meant. Her mind couldn't help but shift to Sebastian's declaration that this man had an interest in her. She examined him a bit more closely as she thanked him. He wasn't terrible to look at. Not anywhere near Sebastian, of course, but who was?

"Will you escort me down?" she asked.

"I'd be honored," Lanford said, and offered his elbow to her.

She took it and felt...nothing. No spark of awareness, no tingle of attraction. That was disappointing. But perhaps something like that could grow if one tried hard enough? Wasn't that possible? Hadn't it been that way with Sebastian?

No. She had to be honest with herself if no one else. She had *always* been aware of Sebastian, even when she'd been too innocent to label what that connection meant. She'd always watched him and longed for him and wanted him to *see* her. When he did? Oh, it was like fireworks on the Thames.

"I hope we'll have a chance to dance together later, my lady," Lanford said as he released her to her brother, who was already waiting in the foyer, doors thrown open to the guests who were starting to arrive on the crushed stone drive. "Unless...unless you prefer another partner."

She blinked as she realized what he was truly asking. He wondered if she was interested in another man. And oh, how she was. But Sebastian was not a road that led to anywhere except pain. Passion, but pain. So she had to turn away, didn't she? That's what he kept telling her. Perhaps now was the best time to start.

"There is no partner in particular that I'm seeking," she said.

"And I'll certainly save a spot on my dance card, Mr. Lanford. In fact, I-I look forward to it greatly."

Something lit up on his face and he gave her a slight bow. "Then I'll find you as soon as the ball begins. Good evening."

He turned and went toward the parlor where the guests would gather before supper. She found Finn watching her closely as she took her spot next to him just as the first family from the shire entered the foyer. They greeted them and a few more early comers. It wasn't for a quarter of an hour before they were alone and her brother faced her slightly.

"Are you well?" he asked gently.

She was startled by the question. Was she allowing her emotions to be so obvious? That wouldn't do. Finn was too clever, and too protective, for that.

"Of course," she said. "I'm only concerned about the gathering going well. The welcome ball is so important to your connections both in London and in the local area."

"You've never let me down, Marianne. You never could." He took her hand and squeezed gently. His expression was filled with love for her as he said, "I know this isn't always easy for you."

She blinked at tears at that admission. Finn couldn't truly understand how she felt about her position in life. He, unlike her, was golden, so he had been untouched by all the gossip caused by their past. But she appreciated the effort nonetheless. She smiled at him for assurance. "Well, perhaps one day soon you'll find some lovely young lady to make your countess and then I'll have a friend in the planning. Or she'll take over entirely."

His cheek twitched as he turned his attention back to the arriving parties. "I'm sure at some point I'll wed. Duty and all."

They refocused their attention on the increasing number of arriving guests and for a long while there was no break in their duties. When the groups began to thin, she glanced over her shoulder toward the hallway. "What do you think of Mr. Lanford, Finn?"

Finn had been staring off into the distance as if distracted, but now his attention snatched to her. "Lanford, eh?" he pressed, though his tone was noncommittal. "He escorted you down, I saw."

She nodded. "We merely bumped into each other at the top of the stairs. But we've spent a little time together since the Brighthollow ball a few weeks ago."

"Yes. I noted that." He shifted slightly. "He seems a fine enough fellow. Sebastian insisted I invite him along to shoot this afternoon and he was companionable enough."

"Sebastian did?" she said softly, wondering why he would do so when it was evident that Sebastian thought little of the man. Unless it was to keep Lanford from her. But that was silly. "Well, I'm glad to hear you have nothing bad to say about him."

Another set of guests passed through the foyer, saying their greetings, shaking hands. As they were escorted by servants to the parlor, Finn sighed. "Rather boring, though, isn't he?"

"Lanford?" She looked at him. "I would guess most people would label me the same way."

He pivoted now and faced her full on. "You? No, *you* are brilliant and witty and insightful."

She blinked at that sharp defense of her character. "I...thank you, Finn."

He took her hand. "Mari, if anyone thinks you are boring, they don't deserve you. And if you think they are, the same is true. You needn't ever settle. I would always take care of all your requirements so that you can retain whatever level of freedom is best for you. I'd rather do that than see you in a miserable marriage. Than see you wither on the vine like our poor mother did."

She pursed her lips. She and her brother had long ago stopped talking about their mother. About their father. Those topics were too sharp. Too painful for each of them and somehow they had never allowed themselves to lean together through that pain.

Which put her to mind of Sebastian. As much as she knew he needed her brother, Finn needed him just as much. If she loved them, as she so very much did, she couldn't separate them by demanding something from Sebastian. Not that she was bold enough to do so.

A last couple entered the foyer and they welcomed them. Then Finn nodded to their butler and said, "If there are any more late comers, escort them to the parlor. We'll take a quarter of an hour there and then be ready for supper."

"Certainly, my lord. I'll ensure the kitchen is aware and let you know if there are any issues with the timeline."

As Bentley slipped away, Finn took her arm and smiled down at her as he led her toward the parlor and its laughter and music within. "I think you and I have both been out of sorts lately due to various troubles," he said. "And I want you to swear to me one thing tonight, Marianne."

"What is that?" she asked with a smile at his light tone and playful wink.

"That you'll have *fun*," he said. "You deserve that."

Then they entered the parlor where all their guests were gathered and separated to mingle amongst them. But as Marianne drifted into the crowd for the duties she never felt quite equipped for, she couldn't help but look for Sebastian and think that if she was going to truly have fun, it could only be with him.

And likely in ways her brother would never approve of.

Sebastian hadn't been able to take his eyes off Marianne all night. He tried to mask his interest, tried to continue talking to the other guests and responding when appropriate, but it felt like a losing battle. They'd been seated at opposite ends of the table at supper. That was usual, he always sat beside Delacourt at these events and Marianne took the place at the other end of the table that would one day be occupied by his friend's countess.

But tonight Sebastian had kept watching Marianne. Watching

who she spoke to, whether she laughed. Did she look engaged by the gentleman to her left? Was he flirting with her?

And now, with the ball in full swing around them, he still couldn't take his eyes off of her. She hadn't missed a dance yet and she'd begun the night in the arms of Lanford. They'd smiled at each other, chatted throughout their turn, she'd laughed like the man was a talented bard.

And then she'd followed with another man and another and another. The men had become faceless, nameless to him, but Marianne had almost begun to glow. She transformed into this unreachable thing he wanted so much that he could almost feel his pulse in every part of his body.

This unreachable thing he had refused for both their sakes. She never looked at him. She never sought him out.

"You look sour, my friend," Delacourt said as he sidled up to Sebastian and handed over a drink. "I got you one that isn't watered down like the punch."

Sebastian forced a smile to his friend and sipped the offered drink. "Did I look sour? I feel nothing like it."

"Hmmm," Delacourt murmured softly. For a moment they simply stood in companionable silence and then the earl sighed. "Marianne is making another splash."

Sebastian looked toward her and tried to pretend like he hadn't noticed her. "Is she? Oh, yes, I suppose she has been dancing all night."

"Never the same partner twice and never against the wall as usual," Delacourt said. "It seems her lot is changing. I should be happy for her, and I am."

Now Sebastian faced him. "But?"

Delacourt was quiet for a long moment, his expression long as he tracked his sister. "It's been so long for her that I fear she'll settle. She asked about Lanford tonight. And if the way he watches her is any indication, the man seems to have a valid interest in her. I must believe he'll approach me with a request to court her at some point. And she'll likely agree."

Sebastian found his breath coming shorter, like he couldn't draw full air into suddenly aching lungs. "I see," he choked out. "What are your thoughts on that?"

"He seems fine enough, I suppose." Delacourt shrugged, as if resigned. "And I understand her desire to wed, to have a family, even if I think the man isn't matched to her wit by half."

Sebastian found he was nodding, like a children's toy on a spring. He couldn't stop as he looked across the room and found Marianne standing with a small group of ladies from the shire...and the very man who was the topic of Delacourt's conversation with Sebastian. Lanford stood at her side, smiling down at her as she spoke.

Sebastian wanted to vomit suddenly and he turned away. "Excuse me, Delacourt, I need a bit of air."

He strode away without waiting for his friend's response and shoved through the crowd, unable to see or hear anything around him over the rush of blood to his ears and the throb of his pulse through every tingling limb of his body.

He burst onto the terrace and gasped in a lungful of cool night air, but it changed nothing. The pressure in his chest still loomed, tension blooming through him that he didn't want to identify or name. He had no right to his feelings, not when he'd made clear to Marianne that there could be nothing between them.

And yet they were there despite that. Those feelings over-whelmed him, seemed to touch every inch of him just as she had the night before. There was jealousy, there was pain, but mostly there was grief. He grieved for something he had never had, or at least claimed he didn't want.

There was a burst of laughter from farther down the large terrace and he glanced down to find a small group of people standing together, drinking their punch and chatting. He resented their ease, that they didn't know he felt like he was being picked apart at poorly stitched seams.

He turned away from them so they wouldn't call out and force him to join their group and hustled down into the darkness away from the ballroom lights that filtered onto the terrace. There was a parlor attached to this same wide terrace and he prayed the door would be unlatched as he reached it.

To his great relief, it was, and he slipped inside into the chamber. The fires weren't lit in here, so the only light came from the beams of moonlight outside. He was just as happy. He didn't want the world to be bright when he felt this way. He just wanted to hide. Hide from his feelings, hide from himself.

He crossed to the darkened fireplace and leaned both hands on the mantel, sucking in deep breaths as he tried to calm himself. But his mind kept spinning back to what Delacourt had said in the ballroom. That Lanford, despite what he'd told Sebastian earlier in the day, was still interested in a courtship with Marianne.

And that she would allow it. Of course, it would lead to marriage if she did. Eventually she might consider what she'd done with Sebastian as merely a lark. Or worse, a regret. His stomach turned with that thought.

"Sebastian?"

He froze, his head still bent, at the sound of Marianne's voice coming from the same terrace door he'd just entered. Was he imagining her in this moment of great upset? Or was she really here? Had she followed him?

Which was worse?

He slowly lifted his head and looked across to the doors. She was standing there, gently pulling them shut behind her so that they would be alone.

He shook his head. "Why are you here, Marianne?" he asked, and hated that his voice was so rough.

"I saw you leave the ballroom," she said after a small hesitation. "You looked upset so I followed."

"You shouldn't have done that," he said.

She stepped toward him and he almost groaned but somehow managed to keep the reaction in check. "We're still friends, aren't we? I still care for you."

He choked out a pained laugh. "Despite it all, eh? Well, I doubt I've acted in a way that deserves it. I promise you, I'm well, Marianne. You should return to the party. You were clearly enjoying yourself and I'd never take that away from you."

She stared at him. He couldn't see her expression clearly in the shadows of the room, but he felt her compassion nonetheless. So often she had showered him with that over the years. Never pity. Always gentle acceptance and kindness and...and care.

She stepped closer again and reached out to take his hand. She had stripped off her gloves at some point and he rarely wore them himself, so her soft skin brushed his just as it had the night before. "I cannot bear seeing you so troubled, Sebastian," she whispered. "Please won't you tell me what brought this on?"

He smelled her in the darkness, that lemony essence that had begun to drive him wild. He wanted to drown in it in this moment. To forget that she might give herself to someone else. That it was his own fault if she did.

"If you cannot bear to see me this way," he said, his breathing harsh now, "I suggest you go."

"No," she whispered, and clung to his hand more tightly. "I won't."

He shook his head. He was swiftly losing any grip on control when she touched him, even in a benign way. When it was gone, he would let words come from his mouth that he wouldn't be able to take back. He would perhaps do things that would bring them both pleasure, but he knew now would also wash him away in greater pain later. At least until he could forget that watching her with another man tore him apart.

"Did you and my brother quarrel?" she asked. "Or did something remind you of those past hurts we discussed last night?"

He dropped his head. She was relentless. He'd always liked that about her. When she focused on a topic, it wasn't something she released until she was satisfied. And when it was a book or an artist or a piece of history, it was glorious to watch her dissect it.

It felt less so when it was him she was picking at, not realizing fully what was there to unleash.

"It's you," he finally choked out.

Her fingers loosened on his briefly, though she didn't drop his hand. She just stared up at him, shafts of moonlight making her eyes look soft and dreamy. "M-Me?" she repeated.

"Yes," he growled, and he placed the hand she wasn't holding against the bare skin of the side of her neck. He traced the line there gently and loved how she trembled with reaction to his touch, how her pulse fluttered in reaction. "You, Marianne."

"How could that be possible?" she whispered.

"Because I see you with him, with all those *hims* out there, and I feel this gnawing ache in me."

"Sebastian," she whispered, almost with no voice.

But he couldn't stop now. The bottle was uncorked. "I feel this *tormenting* desire to push you into a corner and remind you that *I'm* the one who made you shudder with pleasure not even twenty-four hours ago. And I hate it, Marianne. I hate feeling this way. I hate wanting to do that, *needing* to touch you so I can remind *myself* that you were mine once. So if you are as intelligent as I know you are, you'll go. Please, Marianne. Just go."

CHAPTER 19

Marianne couldn't move as Sebastian's rough words washed over her like a caress. In the darkness of the parlor, in the shadows, his confession felt raw and powerful. It overwhelmed her because she felt not only his desire for her still pulsing beneath the surface, but something deeper. Something that called to the love she felt for him and gave her hope she knew would only lead to despair.

And it didn't matter. She couldn't do as he asked. She couldn't walk away and pretend this draw didn't exist and that it wasn't undeniable.

She shivered as she edged a little closer, hearing his breath catch in the dark when her body brushed his. She lifted up on her tiptoes slowly and wrapped her hand around the back of his neck to urge his lips to hers. There was a moment when he didn't move, but then he did, relaxing toward her. When they met, the kiss was so gentle that she nearly burst into tears right there.

She didn't want to do that, so she traced his lips with her tongue and he made a deep, guttural moan before his arms clasped around her and he molded her hard to his chest. He drove his tongue into her mouth, almost punishing, like he could make her run away with his passion if not with his request.

Of course that wasn't true. The passion only inspired her more. She lifted against him, desire washing over her the same way it had the night before. But now she knew what she wanted, she knew what would happen. There was no longer a rising, faceless fear when she touched him, but a wonderful anticipation of the wave that she knew would at some point sweep her into pleasure.

She wanted that. Nothing else mattered in that moment. At least not to her. But perhaps it did to him because he broke away from her at last, pressing his forehead to hers.

"This isn't fair," he whispered, and his voice cracked.

She wrinkled her brow. Did he mean for her? Or for himself? She traced his cheek with her palm and he turned his face into it to kiss the skin there, sending ripples of sensation through her entire body. "What isn't fair is wanting you so much, Sebastian. I want you so much. And I can feel you want me."

He let out a ragged breath before he tucked her a little closer and she did, indeed, feel the evidence of his desire pressed hard and heavy against her stomach. She ached for it and for him.

"It's private here," he murmured, she thought more to himself than to her. "No one knows we came to this room. No one saw."

She realized he was convincing himself and so she kept her mouth shut so she wouldn't disrupt him.

"It's dark," he continued. "Only shadow, almost not real. We could pretend we're not us, just two lovers who found each other and couldn't resist."

She shivered at that idea, even as she looked up into the dark shape of his face. "Sebastian, I could never pretend you aren't you. Never."

He hesitated a moment and she thought perhaps she'd brought him back to reality. That he would push her away and deny them both. But instead he bent his head again and his mouth found hers. His kiss was sweet, burning against her as their tongues tangled in the silence of the room. She was swept up in him, washed away and she knew, just as she knew her own name, that this would happen. He wouldn't deny her.

And she ached for what they were about to share. His hands found the buttons along the back of her gown, slipping them free even as he continued kissing her. She did the same on his jacket and the waistcoat beneath, pushing them both at once so she could get to bare skin faster.

He chuckled at her ardor and shrugged the fabric away before he tugged her dress forward and then traced the line of her throat with his tongue. The trail he made was like fire and she moaned at the pleasure of the sensation. She buried her fingers into his thick hair, arching against him as he sucked and licked.

She tugged down the straps of her chemise and then pulled his shirt from his trouser waist. When she'd unbuttoned enough buttons he released her long enough to yank the shirt off his head. They stared at each other. She was naked from the waist up. He was only in his trousers and boots, his hard cock pressing against the straining buttons of his fall front.

She kept the fleeting eye contact the darkness allowed as she reached out and flicked those buttons open too. The fabric fell to reveal him briefly in the shadowy moonlight.

He tugged her back into his arms, naked flesh against naked flesh now. He was hot as a fire, his hands roving over her back and hips even as he drew her toward the settee across the room. He fell back into a slouched, seated position there and she tumbled across him, her mouth seeking his with increasing desperation and heat. She ached for this, for him, and nothing else mattered now.

He seemed to feel the same. He shifted her position roughly, pushing her skirt up around her hips and helping her straddle his lap. He rocked her against him as his kiss deepened. She felt the heat of him between her legs, nudging the slick entrance to her body as she ground down and felt the echo of the pleasure she knew would come if she let it.

There was no stopping it now. This was fated. She knew it as she shifted and reached between them to position him at her entrance. He grunted as she eased down, his cock sliding easily into her body. There was no discomfort this time, no confusion at the idea that he would claim her. There was only the thick, luscious stretch of his hard body into her softness.

"Oh my God," she moaned, gripping his bare shoulders.

He tugged her down, his tongue meeting hers as she began to grind against his lap in desperation, seeking pleasure without thought, connection without words. He slipped his hands beneath her skirt and cupped her backside, slowing her movements, drawing out the building pleasure.

She savored it, grinding in circles against him, gripping him as she used him. He let her, lifting gently, never taking over even though he could have at any moment. After that had gone on for what felt like a blissful eternity, she broke her mouth from his with a gasp. She tilted her head back over her shoulders, her eyes squeezed shut as she focused on the ripples of pleasure that had already begun.

She felt his breath against her nipple and then his tongue, and it was enough to push her over the edge. As he sucked hard, she fell, groaning while her hips rocked out of control against him.

"Don't stop," he growled against her skin. "I want all of it, Marianne."

She clung to him, her nails digging into his shoulders, her body clenching so tight that she feared she might hurt him. But when she managed to open her eyes, she didn't see pain on his face. Oh no, it was pure pleasure as he watched her at the height of her release. Like he was studying some beautiful painting and trying to memorize each brush stroke.

But at last the pleasure began to soften, fade, and she collapsed against him, her breath short, her forehead pressed to his. He continued to lift beneath her, his hands digging into her backside as he took her.

"I want to come inside of you," he whispered, the words

somehow darker and more erotic when she couldn't fully see his face. "I want you to feel me dripping down your thighs while you're dancing with some other man later tonight."

She rocked against him at that wicked thought.

"But I can't," he said softly, and he pushed her back, sliding her off his cock and back onto his thighs before he came between them.

Without thinking, she reached between them, running her fingers through the evidence of his pleasure and then slipped her hands to her thighs, rubbing the essence of him there, sticky and hot.

"Now we'll both know," she whispered.

"Christ," he muttered, and then pulled her back hard to him and crushed his mouth to hers. "We'll just stay here. I'll fuck you all night. I'll leave your legs shaking so you can't ride for a fortnight."

She nodded against him, arching as he rolled her onto her back and covered her, his mouth desperate against hers. "Yes. All night. All day tomorrow. All week."

He moaned against her skin, his hands pressing to her flesh like he wanted to mark her in some way. She didn't know what would happen next. Despite the pleasures they had both experienced, she felt no cooling of his ardor, nor of her own. Perhaps they *would* have spent all night doing wicked things to each other, bringing pleasure until they were both wrung out from it.

But there was no chance to discover if that were true. Because the door to the chamber came open in that moment and Finn entered the room, with Bentley on his heels.

"No, I'm not certain where she went, she's—"

Her brother cut himself off as he looked across the room to see Sebastian hurling himself in front of Marianne's half-naked body to block her from being seen so undone. She cowered behind him, turning her face into his back as she clawed to raise her chemise. She was shaking so hard, she could hardly keep the fabric in her hands.

Perhaps Finn wouldn't know it was her, perhaps the dark would offer her some protection. Perhaps he'd just think Sebastian had been imprudent with some other lady in attendance and would excuse himself without further inquiry. That had happened before, hadn't it? Neither of them was a monk and it seemed to never change their feelings toward each other.

But that wasn't meant to be. For a moment the chamber was deathly quiet and then she heard her brother's voice, shaking with rage, "Marianne?"

"Delacourt…" Sebastian began, his tone warning, pleading.

But Finn didn't allow him to finish whatever he'd say to try to excuse the shocking scene before them. He simply came across the room, eyes blazing, and punched Sebastian in the mouth, sending him tumbling off the settee onto the floor below.

CHAPTER 20

Sebastian and Delacourt had sparred dozens of times over the years. He knew how hard his friend could punch. As he sat on the floor, jaw aching, Sebastian stared up at him.

"That was the best punch you've thrown in years."

"Don't try to joke your way out of this," Delacourt said, his voice deceptively quiet. "Bentley, get out. Say nothing of this, do you understand?" He hadn't even looked over his shoulder, keeping his glare on Sebastian.

Sebastian saw from the corner of his eye that Marianne had begun to lift her dress up over her chemise, cheeks flaming as she refused to look at anyone in the room. But at least she was covered, at least this wasn't as awful as it could have been.

"Yes, my lord," Bentley said, his voice shaking as he exited the room and shut it behind him.

"Finn," Marianne began.

"Don't say a word until you've fully dressed," Delacourt growled at her, then said to Sebastian, "Get up, you foul fuck, and turn your back so my sister may have some privacy."

Sebastian stood as he'd been told and fastened the flap his trousers. He'd so desperately wanted to remove them not a moment before so that he could feel Marianne's legs tangling with his as he drove into her, her body writhing beneath his. But now he was happy it took so little to recover himself to some acceptable level.

He turned his back. Delacourt was standing just in front of him and he did the same. Sebastian's heart sank. His friend's shoulders were rolled forward, trembling with rage. He could feel the heat of that emotion coming off of Delacourt in waves. And there was nothing he could say or do to change it.

"I need help buttoning," Marianne said softly. "Sebastian, will you?"

Delacourt pivoted and launched himself forward. "There is no way in hell that Ramsbury is going to button your dress, Marianne."

Sebastian tensed, waiting for her to burst into tears or bow her head in the face of her brother's anger. But instead she folded her arms, the gap of her dress increasing with the motion. Delacourt pursed his lips and lifted his gaze to the ceiling.

"Then we're at an impasse," Marianne said in a remarkably calm tone considering the circumstances. "You have ordered me to dress. I cannot do it by myself. I doubt you want to go calling for servants to come in and have even more of them see what you've witnessed. And I have no interest in *you* buttoning my clothing, Phineas. I assume you don't either. It seems a bit too intimate for siblings, does it not?"

Delacourt's expression twisted and he threw up his hands. "Fine, bloody hell, let him button you." He stepped forward. "But I swear on everything that is holy, Ramsbury, if you go too far—"

"I think we can all agree it's a bit late for that," Sebastian said softly. "And I have no intention of doing anything untoward to Marianne with you glaring daggers into my soul."

He stepped forward to Marianne as Delacourt turned away a second time. Although she was putting on a tough front, as he neared her, he saw the glimmer of tears in her eyes. He wanted so much to take her hand, to comfort her. Instead he cupped her elbows, squeezing gently before he turned her so he could button her dress.

"Do everyone a favor, Delacourt, and light some lamps or set the fire. I doubt you want to have whatever conversation is coming next in the dark."

"No, we only soil things in the dark, don't we?" Delacourt grunted. "You only sneak around in the dark ruining my sister."

"Oh, Finn, light the fire, for heaven's sake," Marianne said, her voice trembling.

Sebastian ignored Delacourt now, focusing only on Marianne as he fastened her dress swiftly. When Delacourt moved away, he allowed himself to swiftly touch the exposed skin just below her neck where her chemise began.

"I'm sorry," he said softly.

"It was both of us," she whispered back. "And I know you have far more to lose."

"Stop whispering, you two," Delacourt said, the wood hitting the grate with a crash that made Marianne jump.

Sebastian buttoned the last button and stepped away. Marianne drew a long breath and he was close enough to hear it shaking, then she returned to the settee where he had made love to her, where he had surrendered himself in ways he didn't think he'd ever done.

She blushed as she took her place there, but there was a regal quality to her expression as she looked at her brother and waited, wordless, for whatever punishment would come. Sebastian straightened his back and decided to do the same. If she could behave with such courage, he had to at least try to be as worthy of her as he could be.

The light in the room lifted as Delacourt finished with the fire and then lit a few lamps. Only then did he truly look at his sister. Sebastian did the same. She was still flushed from some combination of pleasure and humiliation. Her hair was mussed from his fingers, from the way she'd thrown her head back as she rippled around him in pleasure.

She had never been so utterly beautiful. How he wanted to keep her like this forever, mussed by his ardor, locked away where they would never be interrupted.

"I'm doing my best not to shout and draw the attention of over fifty people gathered in our ballroom," Delacourt said through clenched teeth. "So I will ask that you two do not trifle with me, do not lie to me. What the hell is going on that I would find you in such a situation?"

Sebastian glanced at Marianne, but she wouldn't look back at him. She stared at her brother, chin lifted. Her pain was just at the surface, despite her attempts to remain strong. Sebastian wanted so desperately to ease it.

"You know how I am—" he began.

Marianne pushed to her feet. "He didn't know it was me."

"What?" Sebastian and Delacourt said at once, both staring at her.

She smoothed her hands over her skirt and nodded. "It's…it's true. I saw Sebastian come into the room from the terrace and I followed him. He must have been expecting someone else, but it was so dark that when he kissed me, he didn't know it was me. I let him, Finn. I know I'll be a spinster forever and I let him without ever revealing myself. I tricked him into what happened, so you shouldn't blame him."

Sebastian stared at her, mouth dropping open in shock. Marianne would sacrifice herself for him? Try to save a friendship that she knew meant the world to him, and in the process possibly damage her own relationship with Delacourt?

"Marianne," Delacourt whispered, his gaze shifting to Sebastian with confusion now. "Is this true?"

She opened her mouth to say yes, still offering Sebastian that lifeline. But he couldn't allow it. He couldn't dismiss her like this lie would require. He couldn't pretend that this hadn't been something with more meaning than a dark, anonymous passion that horrified him when he saw the truth. He *wouldn't* pretend that, consequences be damned.

"It's *not* true," he said softly.

"Sebastian." She stepped toward him, hand outstretched as if she would touch his hand like she had so many times in quiet comfort. "Don't. Don't."

He shook his head. "You are too good, Marianne. Too good for me, certainly. I won't let you do this."

Delacourt stared from her and back to Sebastian. "So she lied."

"To protect me," he said. "Yes. What you walked in on is exactly what you think it was. I engaged in ungentlemanly behavior with your sister. I knew the consequences to our friendship if you were to find out. I did it anyway because my attraction toward her was irresistible."

Marianne's breath caught and she stared at him in surprise. He shifted beneath the powerful emotion that was unguarded on her face in that moment. And he knew Delacourt saw it too. His lips pinched.

"He took advantage," Delacourt said, the anger rolling from him once again.

She shook her head. "*Never.* Never once. I know it's hard for you to see me as a woman with feelings and needs and a heart," she said. "But I *am* those things, Finn. I didn't want to live my life like Claudia did, to reflect only on regrets and missed opportunities when I'm at the end and looking back. Sebastian has been my friend for so long. And I've...I've cared for him as more than a friend for nearly as long."

Sebastian tensed. She wouldn't look at him and yet it felt like she was reaching into his heart and squeezing.

She continued without ever knowing her effect on him. "What happened between us was between two adults. It has nothing to do with you, Finn. It has nothing to do with your friendship."

"Bloody hell it doesn't," Delacourt snapped. He shook his head. "God, I don't even know what to do. I never imagined my maiden sister would crawl into the lap of one of the biggest rakes in England."

Marianne drew back, her dark eyes flashing briefly. "Oh, I'm sorry, is it so hard to believe that I might have some daring in my soul? That I might want more than to be some man's consolation prize as a bride? That I might *want* to feel the things I felt in Sebastian's arms?"

Delacourt flinched and turned his head. He let out his breath shakily. "Go up to your chamber, Marianne," he said softly. "I'll explain to those at the party that you were stricken with a headache. The result of all your hard work to make this ball so successful, no doubt."

"You're banishing me," she said, tears filling her eyes that broke Sebastian's heart because they were his fault.

"No." His tone became gentler, and for that Sebastian was happy. "I'm allowing you a chance not to have spying eyes on you when your hair is half down thanks to him. Not to be forced to pretend that this untenable situation hasn't happened. And giving myself an opportunity to calm down before we speak about this again." He moved forward. "Please, Mari. Just go."

Sebastian turned his head. He'd asked her to do the same not an hour ago. She'd refused. Refused to leave him, refused to pretend like what was happening between them wasn't real and powerful. She was far braver than Sebastian.

However, she listened to her brother this time and only gave Sebastian one more glance before she marched from the room with her head held high. He noticed she left the door open behind herself.

"Still protecting you, it seems." Delacourt rolled his eyes as he went to the door and shut it himself. When he turned back, he leaned against the barrier and shook his head. "You betrayed me. Betrayed my singular request of you."

"I did," Sebastian said, because he could deny none of it.

Delacourt shook his head and his mouth turned farther down. "That's all you have to say?"

"Is there anything I could say?" Sebastian asked.

Now that Marianne was gone and he no longer felt the drive to protect her, the truth of this situation became more and more clear. And increasingly painful. Delacourt could hardly look at him now and when he did it was with an expression heavy with disgust.

"I don't know." Delacourt threw up his hands. "For years and years, I have stood by you. I never judged your worst impulses. Hell, I sometimes indulged in them. I knew who you were, or at least I thought I did. And I asked you this one thing, out of respect for me and our friendship."

"I know," Sebastian said softly.

"So tell me you regret doing this, tell me you're sorry you did something that will change our friendship irrevocably."

Sebastian opened his mouth. He *should* apologize for those things. He should guard the friendship that had saved his life over the brief affair that had left him open to all this. But he couldn't.

"I'm—I'm not sorry that I touched Marianne," he said. "I am sorry you are betrayed by it."

Delacourt stared at him for what felt like an eternity, his gaze narrow and even. Sebastian braced to be hit again, but instead, Delacourt turned away. "In the morning, you'll leave at dawn. I don't care where you go, but you won't be here. I'll make some excuse about an emergency that called you away."

Sebastian bent his head. "I understand."

"You won't crow about this conquest, do you understand?" Delacourt stepped up to him, and there was no denying the seriousness in his tone or his face. "If you *ever* make this public, I will rip your heart out."

Sebastian almost laughed. Delacourt had been the only person in the world who ever thought he had a heart to extract. And Marianne. Marianne had always believed it. She'd made *him* believe it. Now he was losing both of them.

"I'd never hurt your sister in that way."

"Just in every other way that matters," Delacourt muttered, and turned to leave the room.

"Don't be hard on her," Sebastian called out. "She doesn't deserve that."

Delacourt froze at the door and slowly turned back. His nostrils flared slightly and he let out a long, shuddering sigh. "No," he agreed softly. "She doesn't."

Then he left the room and shut the door firmly behind him, leaving Sebastian to bend to get his shirt and put it back on. He did so slowly, his heart aching as what had happened fully sank in. He'd lost his best friend.

And he realized with a start, as he gathered up the rest of his abandoned clothing, that he wasn't thinking entirely about Delacourt. He'd lost Marianne, too, and *that* was what caused his chest to ache, his eyes to sting and his hands to shake as he slipped from the room to begin the packing that would be required for him to sneak off into the dawn tomorrow like the thief he was.

CHAPTER 21

"My lady? My lady?"

Marianne opened her eyes with a start and stared up at Hannah, who was standing over her with a candle. The light haloed her face and gave her a ghostly appearance.

"Goodness, what is it, Hannah?"

"I'm sorry to wake you," her maid said.

Marianne sat up. She was shocked she could *be* awakened. She had hardly slept all night, tossing and turning as she relived both the passionate moments with Sebastian in the parlor and the horrible ones with Finn after. But she must have dozed off at some point.

"Is something wrong? Oh God, did my brother call Sebastian out for pistols?"

"No, my lady, but...but..." Her cheeks darkened. "Lord Ramsbury's carriage is being packed and his horse is being readied."

Marianne threw the covers back and got to her feet, searching for her dressing gown before she exited the room and raced downstairs.

When she reached the foyer, she found Sebastian there, talking quietly to his servants as Bentley stood by, stone faced and arms folded like some kind of ancient guard dog who occasionally remembered he had teeth. No one had seemed to notice her until she said, "Sebastian."

He froze and then turned toward her. His blue eyes met hers, filled with emotion for a brief moment before he cleared it all away. Without looking at his servants, he said, "Go ahead and do as we've discussed. I'll see you in London tomorrow evening."

His servants departed, but Bentley remained, his gaze focused on Marianne in horror, likely at her state of dress given that she was in her dressing gown with no shoes and her hair tangled around her shoulders. Of course, he'd seen worse and that memory made Marianne's cheeks grow hot.

"Please, Bentley, I need a moment alone with the earl," she said.

"My lady, I do not think that would be wise," the butler began.

"Please!" she repeated, her voice elevating.

Bentley bent his head and then hurried from the foyer, worrying his hands before him.

"He'll fetch your brother, you know," Sebastian said softly. "I know he's awake, I assume he's pacing around his study."

She bent her head. "Of course he'll fetch him, so we only have a moment before he comes. Sebastian, I'm so sorry."

"*You're* sorry?" he said, stepping closer.

She looked up into his eyes and all her fear and worry and heartbreak faded briefly. Strange how he could do that to her, even without trying. He always had, it seemed. Always comforted, always supported, always made her smile when she sometimes wanted to scream.

"Yes," she said. "You wanted me to leave last night—"

"I wanted you to stay," he corrected. "I was glad you stayed."

"Even after everything?"

He cupped her cheek gently, fingers tracing her jawline with featherlight touch. "Even after everything."

"He's sending you away." She blinked at tears. "I've ruined your friendship."

He shrugged. "He's sending me away," he agreed. "And he has every right to do so after what happened. But as for our friendship...I suppose we'll see if there's a way to repair it. The fact he didn't murder me in the middle of the parlor is at least a good sign."

A tear slid down her cheek and he wiped it away with his thumb as he let his gaze flicker over her like he was trying to memorize her. She certainly did the same to him.

"That's enough, you two," came Finn's voice from the hallway.

Marianne turned and was surprised to see her brother didn't even seem angry. Just tired. Like he hadn't slept last night, just as she hadn't. Just as Sebastian likely hadn't.

Sebastian stepped away, his hand dropping from her face at the last possible moment before he smiled at her gently. "I'm glad I got to see you. Goodbye, Marianne."

"No, don't say goodbye," she said, not caring if she was doing this in front of her brother. "Not like it's final."

He glanced toward Finn and sighed. "Then I'll just say, good morning. And we'll see what happens later."

He hesitated and she felt him lean toward her, like he wanted one last touch or kiss. But then he pivoted and strode out the door to the horse waiting for him on the drive. He swung up without a backward glance and then rode away out of sight at the turn of the bend of the drive.

She bent her head when he was gone, her breath short and harsh. She felt her brother's arm come around her, holding her up even though he was the one breaking her heart by sending Sebastian away.

"Come, I suppose now is as good a time as ever to have a discussion about the great deal I've apparently missed beneath my very nose," he said.

She didn't resist as he turned her away from the door and back up the hall to his study. How often had she come to this room in her life? She looked around at its shiny cherrywood bookshelves and wide desk. It had been her father's study, and she'd come here to be lectured and shouted out as a child.

But when Finn had inherited, the room she'd once feared had become far more comfortable. Together they had redecorated the space and made it brighter and more welcoming. They'd sat at the desk to laugh over some friend's silly behavior at a ball or to discuss a book they'd both liked. She'd curled up by the fire, indulging in companionable silence while her brother worked at his ledger and she sewed.

Now she sat in one of the comfortable chairs before the roaring fire and felt the same dread she'd felt when the last earl had ruled with such a cruel and harsh manner.

"I'm sure you wish to tell me about your deep disappointment in my behavior," she said, staring at the dancing flames rather than her brother's face.

He took the seat opposite hers and reached over to take her hands in his gently. He leaned closer and shook his head. "There is nothing on this earth that you could do to ever inspire my disappointment, Mari. Nothing. If anything, I'm disappointed in myself for not seeing what was going on."

She sighed. "Well, we were trying to hide it, so I suppose we were just good at it."

"I'm not talking about your…your…"

"Affair," she supplied. Yes, it was an affair now, after all. It fit Claudia's list in a way she had questioned after her first night with Sebastian.

His nose wrinkled. "I won't call it that. But certainly. That. I'm talking about what you said to me last night. That you wanted to be more some man's consolation prize as a bride, that you had daring in your soul that I didn't see."

"I was angry," she said softly. "But those things are true. I know you see me as some failure on the marriage mart who you must protect like glass. But I'm more than that. I feel the same things any other person feels. I want the same things anyone else does."

He nodded. "I would wager you feel them even more deeply, because you're sensitive and kind and intelligent beyond almost any other person I've ever met." His gaze grew distant a moment, but then he refocused. "If you thought I didn't understand you, or truly thought I ever saw you as a failure, I owe you a most sincere apology."

"I did fail, though, didn't I?" she asked.

"Never." He squeezed her hands gently. "Your poor first two seasons were from matters out of your control. And if someone couldn't see your worth after that, then they didn't deserve you in the first place." He shifted a little. "I can see why the attention of someone like Sebastian would be tempting."

"He didn't seduce me," she said, and hoped he could hear that. "It wasn't a situation where he took advantage. We've always been friends, and then suddenly it was more. I wanted that as much as he seemed to. And we're both adults who made this decision."

He bent his head. "I still can't agree to that statement at present. But I do wonder what that means for Lanford. You were asking about him just last night and he seems to have a genuine interest."

She could have laughed at that statement. "Charles Lanford didn't even notice my existence until the Brighthollow ball when I dared to wear something a little more interesting. Yes, I saw him as an escape route, I suppose, and entertained the idea of a courtship if he asked. But…"

When she hesitated her brother's expression softened. "But you love someone else."

They met eyes and she felt his support down to her bones. Not his misplaced protection or his fear for her, but just his understanding.

"Yes. I do," she said. "And that has nothing to do with what happened between us physically. I think I have loved…loved *him* from the first moment I met him. Even though I've never been under the illusion that he could love me in return."

Finn held out his arms, gathering her in a brief hug that warmed her more deeply than the fire ever could. When he released her, he got to his feet and paced to the window across the room where dawn was brightening in the distance. "I wanted to spare you from this pain."

She shook her head. "But you can't, Finn. Risk is pain, love is pain, life is pain sometimes. It's painful to watch Sebastian ride away and know that what should have been something lovely has instead caused so much upset. It's painful not to have…to have Claudia to depend upon or to laugh with anymore. To whisper every detail of what has happened and see her shock and hear her advice. But I wouldn't trade a day of my friendship with either of them to stop the pain now. Both of them were very much worth it."

"You're so wise," he said.

She smiled at him weakly. "Don't tease."

"I'm not. You are very wise, Marianne. Far wiser than I am sometimes. I'd do well to be more like you. Perhaps I shall try in the future." He shook his head sadly. "But for now, we need to decide what to do today."

"Of course," she said, getting to her own feet. "To break the party up so early would only cause a great deal of questions, especially with Sebastian leaving so suddenly. I'll act as hostess as usual and I promise you that no one shall see anything different about me."

"And what about when we return to London?" her brother asked.

She shrugged. "Assuming you aren't going to force me to marry a man who doesn't love me back—"

"I'd never force you to marry, Marianne. There is no circumstance where I would take your own choices away like that." He smiled at her so gently. "I would *never* put you in the same position as our mother. Create desperation in you like what was created in her."

The love she felt for her brother swelled up in her. "You're my champion, I know that, Finn. And Sebastian and I always knew this was a temporary endeavor. I've never asked for more, he certainly could not want it. So I hope that whatever happens when we return to London will be a renewal of your friendship to him, no matter what silly promises you forced upon him when it came to my ruination."

She could see Finn pondering that and he shrugged. "I think this time away will be good for everyone. We all need some perspective that the next ten days will give. After that, I suppose anything is possible."

She bent her head. She no longer believed that, not when it came to Sebastian at any rate. The magic they had shared was over now. She would love him from afar, as she always had without fully admitting it. And they would move on.

Somehow she had to. Somehow she would find a way.

CHAPTER 22

The ten days since Sebastian had ridden away from Delacourt's home, feeling Marianne watching him with every step, had been the longest of his life. He'd had no concentration during that time, no ability to do anything for more than a few minutes before he was haunted by memories of kissing Marianne, of feeling her ripple around him in pleasure, of being comforted by her, laughing with her, watching her blush and blossom.

He dreamed of trying to find her, but she was always out of his reach. Or he'd get close and someone like Lanford or Delacourt would step into the path and then she'd vanish like smoke. The nights had been so very long, and they had revealed truths to him that he didn't want to see or hear or feel. They'd revealed how deeply he cared for Marianne. It was truly terrifying, because caring meant he could be hurt, that he could hurt her more than he already had.

In short, his stomach turned and his head ached with all the thoughts and feelings he normally so readily suppressed.

"My lord?"

He turned to find Jenkins standing in the doorway to the breakfast room, hands folded before him.

"Yes, what is it?" Sebastian asked, wishing his voice didn't sound so strained. It seemed he could no longer meter his reactions.

"You have a visitor, my lord. It's the Earl of Delacourt."

Sebastian nearly dropped the cup in his hand and slowly swallowed past a dry throat before he croaked, "I see. Please have him join me."

The butler left, and in the few moments Sebastian had to prepare, he set his cup down and paced to the window to stare outside into the garden. He'd assumed Delacourt would come to him at some point. They had resolved nothing at Garringford Corners, after all. And now his old friend had had more than a week to nurse his anger and frustration and betrayal.

But on the bright side, at least Sebastian would hear about Marianne. He would know that she was well after that last desperate parting when she'd stood before him looking so beautiful in her dressing gown and told him she was sorry. *She* who had done nothing wrong ever in all her life.

"I'm surprised not to find you on guard as I enter," Delacourt said as he came into the room.

Sebastian faced him and shrugged. "My jaw recovered from the last punch. If you wished to repeat the action, I'm sure it would do so again."

Delacourt stared at him for a long moment, seeking...well, Sebastian wasn't quite certain of what. He forced himself to remain still under the scrutiny until Delacourt turned to the sideboard that was laden with food Sebastian hadn't touched.

"Are you going to invite me to breakfast?" he asked.

Sebastian stepped forward with a flare of hope suddenly burning in his chest. "I-if you would like, I would very much love to have you. Please, take what you would."

Delacourt was quiet as he loaded his plate with all his favorites. Sebastian had to smile because they had done this so many mornings either before they went to fence or box or shoot. Or after a late night when they were both still half-drunk.

Once Delacourt took a seat, Sebastian picked up his teacup and took the head of the table near his right. Delacourt arched a brow. "You aren't eating?"

"I couldn't, I don't think," Sebastian said. "I'll admit, I've been picturing what this encounter would be like for over a week and breaking bread together was not how I imagined it."

"At first it wasn't how I imagined it either," Delacourt admitted with a shake of his head. "I think I've challenged you to a duel or slapped you in the face a dozen times in my mind."

Sebastian forced himself not to duck away from his friend's gaze. "And is that what you're here to do now, no matter how politely we've begun?"

"No." Delacourt chewed thoughtfully for a moment and said, "I've no intention of dueling you or fighting you."

"Not that I'm not pleased to hear it, but may I ask why?" Sebastian asked. "I'd certainly deserve it."

"Are *you* challenging *me*, old friend?" Delacourt asked before he sipped his tea.

"Never," Sebastian said. "If we were to duel, I think you'd have to shoot me. I would never be able to bring myself to fire upon you."

"That's nice to hear." Delacourt brushed his hands together and then leaned back, draping his elbow over the back of his seat with nonchalance. "I think it would be very difficult for me to shoot you, too. And even if I could, I wouldn't. Because Marianne would never forgive me."

"She would never forgive either of us if we physically hurt each other over her, no. And she's had so much loss lately." Sebastian frowned. "How—how is she?"

"She rallied quite well after you left the estate. Not a one of the gentlemen there ever would have noticed that she was not herself." Delacourt sighed. "None but me. And I suppose you would have known, too, wouldn't you? You would have seen the little shifts in her. The little flutters and frowns and distractions that add up to how her heart breaks."

Sebastian set his jaw at that thought. Marianne with a broken heart. Over him?

Delacourt leaned closer. "May I ask you a question?"

He nodded, still unable to speak.

"Were you truly willing to risk our lifelong friendship over a *dalliance?*"

"Yes," Sebastian said, but it sounded wrong and so he shook his head. "No."

Delacourt's hands clenched on the table. "I think you'll have to make up your mind, *Sebastian*."

He emphasized Sebastian's given name and he jerked his head up to look at his friend. They had stopped calling each other by those when they each inherited. It brought him to mind of long-ago times when they had first become close as brothers.

He cleared his throat. Aside from Marianne, the person he would want to discuss these sorts of topics with most was the very one sitting across from him. Not being able to talk over his confusion and upheaval over the unexpected connection to Marianne had been stifling.

"It...it wasn't a mere dalliance," he said softly.

Delacourt's cheek twitched, but he gave no other physical reaction to that confession. "Then what was it?"

Sebastian closed his eyes and tried to find the words for what he was too afraid to explore in his mind and his heart. He thought of every moment he'd spent with Marianne, not just in the last few weeks, but since he'd first met her. He thought of their friendship and how much it had meant to him even when he tried to play it off as unimportant. He thought of all the times he'd gravitated toward her to hear her opinions or receive her praise. Or even her gentle censure when he deserved it.

He thought of the first time he'd kissed her and the way it had felt so right. Almost like he'd never kissed anyone else before her, which was certainly not true. He thought of how she wound her way into his blood, keeping him up at night with thoughts of her.

"Sebastian," Finn said softly.

He opened his eyes. "I can't name it," he said at last. "I don't know."

Finn pursed his lips slightly, but he didn't look angry at that response. He got to his feet at last and said, "I hope you'll figure it out because you are both miserable and it's hard to watch."

Sebastian followed him to his feet and stared in confusion as Finn strode toward the door. "Finn, wait," he called out.

Delacourt turned back. "Yes?"

"That's all? You have nothing else to say about all of this? No warning me off your sister, no demands that I make things right?"

"As you both told me, you are two adults, well capable of taking care of yourselves. My interference to keep you from her clearly didn't work before. Perhaps it would be best for me to stay out of it now. I hope I'll see you for sparring later in the week. I have a few frustrations that have nothing to do with my sister which I'd love to work out. Good day, Sebastian."

"Good day," Sebastian repeated even though the words almost felt as though they had no meaning as Delacourt departed the room like he hadn't just set off a bomb.

It seemed like his friend was giving permission for whatever Sebastian might like to do. Might dare to do when it came to Marianne. The ban was lifted and for the first time in a long time, Sebastian felt...free.

Only he was left with a thousand questions about what step to take next. What *did* he want when it came to Marianne? More to the point, what could he provide to her after a life of bored dissolution?

"And how does one court a lady, at any rate?" he muttered out loud, and then froze when he heard the words.

Court her. Court Marianne. He'd never courted anyone because courtship had a natural end and it was one he'd always avoided. He didn't want to wed, at least not with emotions involved.

But now he stared at his hands clenched before him, these hands that had held her far too long ago, and he wanted to use them to take care of her for the rest of his life. He wanted to use them to please her and comfort her and support her.

Because he...he loved her? Could that be right? Could this feeling that swelled up when he thought of her, when he feared losing her, when he pictured a life whether it be joyfully with or painfully without her be...love?

He took a hard seat back at the head of the table. That thought was too powerful now. It felt so foreign and yet so absolutely fitting. So perfectly true.

The answer to his initial question became clearer now, too. To court a lady, or at least to court Marianne, he would look to the list he knew she was pursuing. He would give her what she wanted, help her fulfill her dreams and honor her friend. And perhaps in the process, he could also show her that he was a worthy risk to take.

Maybe he would show himself, too. Because in that moment he was afraid that perhaps he couldn't measure up to the remarkable woman who had changed his entire life and now was positioned at the center of it. And he so wanted to do just that. No matter what he had to sacrifice to get there.

CHAPTER 23

Marianne sat at the breakfast table, a plate set before her, and stared into the distance, not seeing any of it. Her mind was too distracted, as it had been for over a week, with thoughts and memories.

"Ah, good morning, Marianne," her aunt said as she shuffled into the room and made herself a plate.

"Good morning, Aunt Beulah," she replied with as large a smile as she could manage. "That yellow is very nice on you."

"Thank you, my dear," her aunt said, and took a seat beside Marianne. She settled a napkin into her lap. "You don't look to have reviewed the invitations we've received since your absence in the country."

She motioned to the tray beside Marianne's right hand, which was, indeed, brimming with invitations to balls and teas. Such a strange thing, really. At some point in her life, Marianne would have been thrilled at the increased attention, but now she looked at the pile with nothing but dread.

"There was so much excitement at Garringford Corners, I suppose I'm just looking forward to a few days of quiet," she said, hoping it would put her aunt off of any idea of attending parties.

"I understand," Beulah said, patting Marianne's hand. They were quiet a moment as they both sipped their tea, then her aunt said, "But I did see an invitation from Lady Wilmington. She's so very influential and I don't think we've ever been invited by her."

Marianne pursed her lips and looked into her aunt's face, which was bright with the excitement over the important offer. "You would like to go."

Beulah reached over and dug through the tray until she found the correct item and pushed it to Marianne. "I think we should, my dear. You clearly have an increased interest at present, we have twice as many invitations as ever—why not take advantage? Plus, I've always wanted to see the famous Wilmington sconces. They say they are decorated with real gems."

Marianne looked over the invitation. "The ball is tonight."

"It is. So you'd have an entire day to rest if you'd like and then dance the night away. Perhaps your Mr. Lanford will even be there. I assume you'd like to see him after you spent time together at the estate."

Marianne arched a brow at her. "Are you matchmaking, auntie?"

Beulah laughed. "Just encouraging you to take advantage of any option you may find."

"Well, Mr. Lanford is not an option," she said gently. "He's very kind but we do not suit, it seems."

"Oh." Beulah sighed. "That's too bad. But still. The *sconces*, Marianne!"

She couldn't help but laugh. "I suppose I couldn't turn down an opportunity to see bejeweled sconces, now could I? Are they diamonds or emeralds or..."

"My understanding is that there is a wide variety of gems." Beulah rubbed her hands together. "I shall write the acceptance to Lady Wilmington right after breakfast and I think you should wear that dark blue gown that Hannah altered so prettily for you recently."

Marianne sighed but nodded. "Of course, Aunt Beulah, I'll do just that. Now, why don't you tell me of your visit with Cousin Fiona? I was sad she wasn't still here when I returned."

"Oh, Fiona," Beulah rolled her eyes and leaned forward with the light of gossip brightening her face. "Let me tell you all about Fiona and her misadventures in Bath before her arrival."

Marianne leaned in, too, trying to lose herself in her aunt's tale of their sweet but slightly featherbrained cousin's attempt to buy a hat in Bath, but her heart sank with every thought of going to a ball tonight. Her heart was certainly not in the exercise. And worse, she feared she might see Sebastian there. All the possibilities of what might happen in this first meeting after everything that had transpired between them was terrifying.

But she supposed it had to happen sometime, so if it was tonight at least that would get the awkwardness over faster and she could start moving on with her life. A life that felt a little duller knowing she wouldn't have those wonderful encounters with the man she loved so desperately.

Lord and Lady Wilmington's London ballroom was impressive, even Marianne could admit that as she trudged into the sparkling chamber at her aunt's side that night. Still, as bright and glorious as the room was, with its sparkling chandeliers and finely liveried servants and the famous sconces dazzling with the candlelight behind them, she felt nothing but dread as the servant announced their arrival.

Eyes turned toward them and lingered a moment, then the groups returned to their discussions. Marianne noticed a few gentlemen tracking her as she made her way through the crush, but she made no effort to connect. She didn't want to attract attention tonight. Claudia's dream to *Fill My Dance Card* was no longer one Marianne wished to share, even if the opportunity was there to finally complete that item.

"I see some friends there," Beulah said.

"Very good," Marianne replied with a brief squeeze to her aunt's hand. "I think I'll just find a place along the wall and gather myself a little."

Beulah nodded and they parted ways. Marianne weaved through the crowd until she reached the wall where she took her old place. She ducked her head so that she would send the message she didn't wish to be bothered and hoped she would fade into the woodwork soon enough.

But just as she was getting comfortable, the footman at the door announced, "The Earl of Ramsbury."

She jerked her head up to watch as Sebastian strode into the ballroom. Her breath caught as she saw him for the first time in what felt like a lifetime. Even from a distance, she was dazzled by him, by how handsome he looked in his formal attire, by how his confidence was clear in every certain step, in every acknowledging bow of his head to friends. He scanned the ballroom, clearly searching for someone. And then his gaze fell on her and she realized it was her he was looking for.

She started to shake as he made his way across the room to her. The attention had to be obvious to those around him, for he entirely ignored everyone else as he made his way to her. Her heart was pounding and she felt out of breath as he stopped before her at last and his blue stare swept over her from head to toe like a caress.

"Marianne," he said.

She tried to recall how to formulate words as she gave a small curtsey. "Sebastian," she whispered back, for she could get no more strength into her voice.

He smiled at her. "I so hoped you would be here tonight. Will you dance with me?"

He held out a hand and she stared at it. The last time she'd touched that hand, it had been smoothing over her naked flesh, arousing and pleasing her in ways she feared she'd never fully feel again except in her most wicked dreams.

"At some point you need to say yes or no, Marianne," he said gently.

She shook her head. "I'm sorry, I was distracted. Yes, I'll dance with you."

He let out what sounded to be a sigh of relief and watched closely as she took his hand. There was a jolt of awareness that moved through her when they touched. It hadn't been so very long since it had last happened, but it felt like a lifetime and she longed to feel his arms come around her in more intimate ways than the country dance they were about to begin would allow.

They took their places in the line of dancers and he smiled at her from across the aisle between them. He looked entirely untroubled, as if the distance between them hadn't been a bother at all. But of course it likely hadn't. He hadn't seen her as anything more than a lover. A person to pass the time with. And yet her heart ached as she looked at him, drank in all the lines of him.

Their first turn down the line came a few moments later and he reached out to take her hands as they did their first skipping steps together.

"I've worried about you incessantly," he said now that they could quietly speak. "And how you fared after my departure to London."

She glanced up at him briefly as he gently turned her and then continued down the line. "And I worried about you. But I assure you that you needn't be concerned. I was well and no one found out about…about everything except for Finn."

They were forced to part then as they took their spot to watch the other couples. Only Sebastian wasn't doing that. He continued to stare at her, his expression more troubled than before. She shifted beneath the focused regard and when it became their turn to meet in the middle of the aisle again, she said, "I appreciate your kindness in asking me to dance, but I understand if you want nothing to do with me after Finn kicked you out of the party."

His brow knitted and his hand was warm on her back as he spun her gently. "He had every right. I behaved badly."

They were parted again and she frowned. There was something like remorse in his tone and she wondered how he felt about everything...about her...truly. They would have one more turn down the line before the end of the song and when it came after what seemed like an eternity, she said, "Does that mean you regret everything that transpired?"

He slightly stumbled in his steps before he said, "No, not at all."

He turned her and they reached the end of the line where the couples all bowed to each other as the music ended. He took her hand and guided her away from the dancefloor, but he didn't part from her, nor release her. "If I were to meet you at my carriage in a few moments, would you go somewhere with me?"

She caught her breath. He was so entirely focused on her and he looked so...earnest. Had she ever seen Sebastian seem so earnest before? Perhaps about cakes, but never a person. Never her. It was intoxicating.

"Where? When?" she whispered.

"Now. Please?" He squeezed her hand gently and she bent her head. What he was asking was entirely inappropriate and could lead to even more problems for them both. Finn had clearly forgiven her transgression and hadn't called Sebastian out, but that didn't mean he would allow them to flout his rules in front of the world.

And yet, in spite of all that, she found herself nodding. "Yes. I'll meet you at your carriage."

"Good. I'll depart now with some excuse. You find your aunt and say you are not well and having a ride home with a friend so she may stay."

"I'm sure she'll believe that, if only because she wants to soak in all of Lady Wilmington's ostentatious wealth."

"Oh Lord, did you see her ridiculous sconces?"

Marianne couldn't stifle a laugh. "They were everything my aunt could have hoped for when she waxed poetic about them. Bejeweled, you know."

"I'll tell you a secret," Sebastian said, leaning closer so that his warm breath tickled her ear and made her body ache with wanting him so. "They're nothing but glass, not a real gem in the lot."

"I knew it!" she said with a giggle, and for a moment everything felt right as she stared up into his handsome face and they laughed together.

His smile fell and he cleared his throat. "I'll meet you with the carriage shortly."

With that he released her and disappeared back into the growing crowd. She shook her head, for she knew she was doing something that could cause trouble. She ought to try to move forward from her affair with Sebastian, because she knew it had no good end. But he looked at her and all she felt was love, an emotion that kept her from being prudent. If she could have one more night with him, whatever that meant, then she would take it.

Consequences be damned.

Sebastian could hardly breathe when Marianne appeared at the carriage door less than half an hour after they parted. He opened it and helped her in. What he wanted to do was tug her across the gap between them and kiss her until she moaned his name.

But instead he kept his hands clenched in his lap. If this all worked out, he would have plenty of time to do exactly what his body ached to do. Right now he had to focus on the plan. On the risk.

"Did you have any trouble?" he asked.

She shook her head. "My aunt was having too good a time to even consider departing early. I think she was even dancing."

"Good for Aunt Beulah," Sebastian said with a laugh. "I've always liked her."

"She likes you," Marianne said.

"You think she still would if she knew I utterly ruined her lovely niece?"

She swallowed and he tracked the way her throat moved, marked the flutter of her pulse there. "Perhaps my aunt has deeper waters than anyone knows. Perhaps she would whisper to me about her own illicit affairs of her youth."

"That would be something remarkable," he said softly, and finally reached out to take her hand. She was still wearing gloves and he frowned because he wanted to feel her skin against his. Her cheeks flamed and she tugged her hand away.

His heart sank. Perhaps she was finished with him. Perhaps the humiliation of being caught by her brother had ended any attraction she had toward him and—

His thoughts faded for she met his eyes and unbuttoned her glove slowly. She tugged the silk away and then placed her hand back into his own, which was bare after he'd removed his own gloves the moment he'd entered the carriage.

Her breath hissed out when their skin touched. He realized it met with his own ragged breath.

"I missed touching you," he whispered in the quiet of the carriage.

She nodded. "I missed it too."

They stared at each other, the tension thickening in the air. Then she dropped her gaze. "Where are you taking me?"

He pushed thoughts of touching her away once again and cleared his throat. Here came the moment. The moment when he would reveal what he knew. Where he would take the first risk in a future he was beginning to want to build with a desperation that overpowered him.

How had he not known he loved her before? How had it not been so clear?

"I'm taking you to a party."

She wrinkled her brow. "What? We were just at a party."

"Yes, but this one you weren't invited to."

Her brow wrinkled and confusion lined her face, but then a glimmer of understanding replaced it.

"That was what was on Claudia's list, wasn't it?" he said softly. "To attend a party to which you weren't invited? And unless you crossed it off in the time we were parted, I think it's something you still must attend to. I'd like to help, if you'd allow me."

CHAPTER 24

Marianne struggled to breathe as she stared across the dimly lit carriage at Sebastian's face. He was waiting for her to respond, but she couldn't, not when information was hitting her from all sides. The most important of which was that Sebastian knew about the list. He *knew*.

She swallowed and slowly withdrew her hand from his, even though to do so made her cold down to her bones. "I don't know what you mean."

He arched a brow. "I see. Well, since I'd like to get past this and to the more enjoyable parts of our evening, let me rush the next conversation. You've denied what I said, so I'll tell you that I *know* absolutely and without doubt. You'll ask me how. I'll shift and stammer because I recognize I did something wrong."

"*Wrong?*" She sat up straighter. "What did you do?"

He tilted his head and his gaze held hers firmly. "The night you went to the hell with Lanford, I *was* looking for you. And I *did* go into your chamber in the hopes we could talk. Honestly, I suppose it was in the hopes we might do more than talk because my body knew what my mind was not ready for."

She wrinkled her brow at that statement, which she didn't fully comprehend. "I—"

He held up a hand. "I'll tell you. I suppose I did *two* wrong things. The first was entering your chamber without permission, the second was looking around when I realized you weren't there. In the beginning, it was only out of curiosity."

She couldn't breathe. She clenched her hands in her lap, staring at him as he stood on the edge of dismantling her entirely. At least that was how dire this moment felt.

"And…and what did you find?" she gasped.

"Marianne," he said gently. "You know what I found. You left the list out on the dressing table. I assume because you didn't expect some ungentlemanly cad like the Earl of Ramsbury to come into your room uninvited. I wouldn't have disturbed it, but I saw my name written in your notes. By the way, being alone with me definitely counts as being unescorted."

She bent her head. "Yes. I wrote that part long before you even kissed me."

"Hmmm." He reached out and took her hand again. Now he linked his fingers through hers and tugged her over to his side of the carriage. When he wrapped his arm around her, tucking her against him, she couldn't help but let out her breath in a shuddering sigh.

"You must have thought me the most ridiculous, pathetic fool when you saw it." She refused to look at him when he gave his answer.

Only he didn't allow her to hide. He slipped a finger beneath her chin and tilted her face up. "Never. Never *once* in all the years I've known you have I ever thought you ridiculous or pathetic and I never shall in all the years to come that I hope our lives will be intertwined."

"Sebastian?" she whispered, her heart leaping at those words. They felt like he was offering a future. Could that be right? Or was he just reassuring her that their friendship was intact, even while he held her like a lover?

He smiled. "I only question why you didn't tell me what was happening. You were using me to assist you in completing the list, that much is clear. Why not just be honest?"

She stared at her hands in her lap, pushing aside the questions his behavior inspired in her, at least for the moment. She was putting her hopes and feelings for him into this charged moment, she couldn't read too much into it. "When Claudia died, I felt so alone. She was my closest friend and confidante. She left me her jewelry box, I'd always admired it. But when I received it, I realized there was something hidden inside."

"The list," he said softly.

"Yes, it was Claudia's to start." Tears stung her eyes. "She was so sick, so suddenly, and she must have been pondering her life. She wrote all these dreams, all these wild hopes of what to do if she lived. And when I saw them I also saw how empty I'd allowed my life to become. All I did was stand at walls, drink tea with other spinsters and sleep. What a sad, slow march to whatever end of my own life that will eventually come."

He winced. "Hopefully not for many, many years."

"I'm sure Claudia hoped that too. And her early loss made me want to-well, I suppose it made me want to do something *now*. And yes, I used you to fulfill a few of those items because I-I trust you, Sebastian."

Now his expression softened and his arm around her grew tighter. "I'm glad I've earned that. Even if I was a snoop in your chamber that night."

"I'll be honest that if I found myself in your chamber alone, I'd likely look at your things, too. And if I discovered something with my name on it, I'd *definitely* look." She sighed. "I was foolish to leave the list out. But I was on my way to meet Mr. Lanford and go to the hell, so I scribbled my note about it and then left it in my haste. And now you know it all."

"Except the answer to my actual question," he said softly. "Which was why you didn't tell me, ask me more directly for help."

"I-I thought you'd say no. I thought you'd tell Finn because you believed it was for my own good to go back into the corner where I belonged." She sighed. "I thought you would think me silly."

He nodded. "You've been relegated into the corner by Society for too long. Not seen by those around you, including me, I'm afraid. But I must tell you how deeply I admire you for trying something so bold."

She laughed. "It cannot seem bold at all to a man who is known for rabble-rousing. My little rebellions cannot be anything to you."

"You're wrong, they're everything." His fingers came up to trace her cheek. "Flouting expectation is incredibly brave. I'm in awe of you. I hope I can be so brave, to be a different kind of man."

She drew back. What kind of man did Sebastian imply he wished to be? She would have asked, but the carriage was coming to a stop and he smiled as he glanced out the window.

"Now we've arrived. But I don't want to force you to do anything that would make you uncomfortable. This is not the kind of party that a lady would often attend, you see. So it will cross something off your list, but if you don't wish to do it, we don't have to."

She stared up at him, memorizing his expression in the dim light from the lamps outside at whatever mystery location he'd brought her to. She didn't need to look at it. Didn't need to ask questions. She merely nodded. "I already told you, I trust you, Sebastian."

He didn't move for a moment but then he lowered his lips. She lifted to meet him and they were kissing for the first time in over ten days. It was like a lifetime and she clung to him in relief that she would know his taste again. He clutched her against his chest, his mouth becoming more hungry, more demanding on hers. She met him for every stroke, pushing herself closer, almost into his lap in the tight confines of the carriage.

But before everything could escalate into the encounter of her foggy, heated dreams, he drew back. He was panting, his rough breaths matching her own.

"Great God, what you do to me," he muttered, she thought more to himself than to her. "But you cannot deter me, though I very much appreciate the attempt."

"*You* kissed *me!*" she burst out with a laugh.

He shook his head. "Me? I'm a perfect gentleman. That cannot be true." He rapped his hand against the carriage wall with a wicked grin.

And that exchange released all the tension between them in a moment. She was smiling as the servant opened the carriage door, and Sebastian exited first so that he could help her. He tucked her hand into his elbow and they turned toward a large, brightly lit estate before them.

"I don't know this place," Marianne said softly as they approached the open door that led into a dazzling foyer.

"I should say not. This is the estate of a woman named Vivien Manning, an infamous courtesan." Marianne's mouth dropped open and he laughed at her shock. "We do not have to stay if you don't wish. But the moment we cross that threshold you'll have attended a party to which you were very much not invited."

She drew in a long breath. "I've nothing to lose, I suppose. Yes, let's go in."

He escorted her forward and they entered the foyer. The servant there seemed to recognize Sebastian, which set off a twinge in Marianne's chest that she didn't particularly like. It would be ridiculous to be jealous of this man's past, especially since he wasn't even hers. Whatever was happening between them now wasn't permanent, no matter how her aching heart wished it to be.

Together they went down a long hallway and Marianne looked around her in wonder. It was a chic, sophisticated home, decorated to perfection. Certainly not what she would have pictured if someone had asked her to imagine the dwelling of an *infamous courtesan*, as Sebastian had called her.

The ballroom doors were all thrown open and in the distance she heard lively music being played. When they entered the room, she caught her breath again. There was some sort of theme being played out it seemed, for all of Miss Manning's servants were wearing scanty livery that made them look like fairies. The guests were wearing something of the same, wings affixed to shockingly low gowns on the ladies and the jackets of the men's best. But other than the increase in bare flesh, it was exactly like a Society ball.

Which Marianne was about to say when they were approached by a beautiful blonde woman with sharp, bright blue eyes. "Ramsbury," she said, her voice light and musical. "I didn't expect to see you here tonight."

"Good evening, Vivien," he said with a slight bow. "It's been too long."

"It has," she said, and her gaze focused on Sebastian's face for what felt like far too long for Marianne's taste. Then she shifted it and those blue eyes met her own. "I do not recognize your friend."

Marianne swallowed. She'd never been an uninvited guest before, but here they were. And she found herself extending her hand. "Marianne," she said simply. "Sebastian's lover."

He pivoted his head toward her, his eyes suddenly wide. She almost laughed at the sight of him. He actually looked shocked and that was highly difficult to do.

Miss Manning smiled. "Then you are most welcome. I hope you'll enjoy the gathering. Good evening, Ramsbury…Marianne."

She gave Sebastian a knowing look and then slipped off into the crowd and left them alone. When she had, he pivoted toward Marianne. "I think you've completed two items from that list of yours. Attend a party to which you were not invited and say something shocking!"

"Is it shocking if it's true?" she asked, although she knew the answer. "I admit I rather liked shocking you."

"I liked being shocked," he said with a laugh. "Keep doing things that are so unexpected and I will not make it through the night before I'll need to get you alone in my carriage again."

He motioned toward the dancefloor and she nodded. As they began to move, she noticed he pulled her far closer than he ever would have done in a Society ballroom. Enough that she felt the full length of his body from chest to hip. She shivered at the warmth of him.

"Are you saying that my being shocking is arousing to you?" she asked.

"Being around you in any way is arousing," he admitted softly, his gaze never leaving hers, even as he guided her around other couples and their protruding wings. "But yes, it's always fun to be set on one's head by a partner. Keeps a man on his toes."

They made a few more turns together and then Marianne sighed. "Was Miss Manning *your* mistress?"

His expression softened. "Are you jealous?"

"I know I've no place to be," she said slowly.

"She was never my mistress," he said, and his fingers tightened against her lower back briefly. "I've had mistresses, of course. A few I even met at Vivien's gatherings. She's known as a sort of match-maker for men and their mistresses. But I haven't had a mistress for a long time, Marianne."

"You haven't?" She sighed. That fact made her feel better, foolish as the reaction was. "Your past is your own, I know. I have no right to demand to know more about it."

"I was jealous of you and Lanford," he said.

"You were?"

"Burning with it," he admitted, and then shocked her by bending his head and pressing his lips to hers gently. It was brief, but the public display still made her blush. When he pulled away, he said, "I wanted to do that in front of him, to lay some kind of barbaric claim on you. Unfair, I know, but no less true. So you're not alone in that unpleasant reaction."

The song they were dancing to ended and the orchestra began with a livelier one. He laughed as he swung her around in time and they fell into the steps. "Come, let's enjoy ourselves. Let's dance and watch the couples and gossip shamelessly about them and drink Vivien's punch, but not too much, because she doesn't water it down."

She couldn't help but smile at his enthusiasm, at his focus on her, at the light of him that made everything that had ever been dark seem...better. And she nodded and fell into the joy of simply being with him. Even if it could lead to nothing, the moment of it was worth any pain that might follow.

So many hours later that he could hardly count them, Sebastian helped Marianne back into his carriage and then joined her, letting her rest her head on his shoulder. It had been a remarkable night. Unlike in Society ballrooms, where he had so often felt her tension, Marianne had allowed herself to be free at Vivien's. She'd danced and laughed, she'd been kind to everyone she met, regardless of their station. She'd blushed when the desires of those around them became clear or when she noticed how naughty some of the wallpaper or art pieces were.

In short, she had been a delight and watching her, being with her, had only strengthened all of Sebastian's resolve. Now he smoothed her hair and said, "Will you come back to my home?"

She lifted her head slightly and her gaze glittered in the darkness. "Go home with you?"

He nodded. "Please. I don't want this night to end. I could teach you billiards. Isn't that on your list?"

She smiled. "You really did read closely. In fact, aside from filling my dance card, I believe learning billiards is the last item on my...*Claudia's* list."

"Then let me help you cross it off. Come home with me."

"Is that the only reason?" she whispered.

The question was bold and he smiled. God, but he loved this side of her. The one that didn't fear the consequences because she trusted him. Because she trusted herself.

"If you would allow me, I'd certainly give you other reasons to stay," he said, and lifted her hand to his lips, brushing her skin gently. "I would make up for the last time we were imprudent and interrupted before I could give you everything you so deserve and more."

"I'll go home with you."

He reached back and knocked twice on the wall and the carriage picked up speed as it headed toward his home. She tilted her head in question.

He shrugged. "I said if I knocked once to take you back to your home. If twice, we'd go to mine."

"An excellent system," she said as she rested her head back on his shoulder.

They were quiet on the rest of the ride to his estate. Normally, he might have felt uncomfortable in such silence, tried to fill it, but with Marianne there wasn't a need. He simply looked at their intertwined fingers, resting against his thigh. It was all so *easy*.

They reached the estate in half an hour and soon enough were inside. He dismissed his butler and any other servants, with Marianne blushing beside him and refusing to meet the eyes of anyone they passed.

"They're discreet," he said as he pushed open the door to the billiards room and motioned her inside.

"I suppose they must be," she said, "over the years. You must have brought many ladies here."

He tracked her as she moved to the billiards table and leaned her hands against the edge, her thumbs brushing the velvet fabric absently. "You've brought up my past and all its rumored lovers twice tonight," he said softly. "Would you like to discuss that further?"

She didn't look up and her cheeks were bright with color. "I'm sure you don't wish to talk about that."

"I've suggested it," he said. "And I'm happy to clear up any misconceptions you might have."

Now she did look up, her expression filled with disbelief. "Misconceptions?" she repeated. "Are you saying you haven't lived your life as a libertine?"

"I have," he said. "Like many a man of privilege, I've often chosen the path of a wastrel. I like pleasure, as I think you know. I've sought it out with lovers and mistresses over the years."

She folded her arms like a shield and he could see that those words hurt her, even if she had already known they were true. Which meant she cared. She cared about him. Loved him, he didn't know. But he could work with caring.

He stepped toward her. "I'll tell you this: those assignations were meaningless emotionally. I never let anyone closer than my body. They were transactional exchanges, on both sides. Pleasure for pleasure and nothing more. I enjoyed myself, I did my best to ensure the lady in question did the same. But when we parted ways, I never, not even once, felt a twinge of longing or regret for what I'd walked away from."

She swallowed. "That sounds very empty."

"It was, though I wouldn't have admitted it to myself." Now he shifted as his fears flooded him. He was about to say things he never believed he'd say. Do something he'd never believed he'd do. And he had no idea how this woman, this remarkable woman, would respond. But he'd do it anyway, because the weight of his heart was greater than the depth of his fear.

"Marianne, the first time I ever felt bereft when I walked away from a woman was when I was asked to leave you behind in Garringford Corners."

The color left her cheeks at that admission and she stared up at him in what could only be described as confusion as those words sank in. "Wh-what?"

He took her hand. It trembled in his own, or was it his that trembled? He couldn't tell anymore. Perhaps it didn't matter.

"Marianne, the last ten days without you have been the worst of my life. All I have thought about, dreamed about, written about is you. All I have wanted in my bed and in my parlors and on my arm, is you. And when you haven't been there, I realized more and more what I cannot live without is *you*."

She tried to step back and he gently held her, not to force her to agree, but because he needed her to know he meant those words.

"I-I don't understand," she breathed, the words almost unrecognizable despite the fact that they were right next to each other.

"Because I haven't been clear," he said. "Too many times, to myself and to you. But I want to be perfectly clear now. I don't want you to misunderstand or be able to question what I meant later when you think about this. I love you, Marianne. I am in love with you."

He waited for her response, waited for joy or discomfort or anything to cross her face. But she simply stared at him, unblinking and for the first time he wondered if he had read this entire situation the wrong way.

Wondered if he was about to lose not just his friend, but the love of his life.

CHAPTER 25

Marianne's ears were ringing and her heart was beating so fast and hard that she feared it might burst from her chest. She stared up at Sebastian, trying to decide if she was dreaming or asleep, if she was mad or sane when she heard him say those words.

"I am beginning to think I've stricken you mute," he said after what felt like an eternity passed. He no longer looked so certain as he always did, but *worried*.

He was worried she didn't return his feelings.

And that shook her back to reality and she gasped in a deep breath. "Are you saying those things out of pity?"

He drew back. "You think I, the ultimate rake, would tell you I loved you out of *pity*? Rather than gnaw off my own arm to avoid ever being trapped by this?"

"I don't know."

"If I pitied you, I'd get you a nice cake, Marianne, I wouldn't declare my heart in the billiards room." He smiled. "I say I love you because it's true. I realize you doubt me, perhaps because you've been so mistreated over the years. Perhaps because I forced myself to keep you as a friend and nothing more until these feelings became too powerful to ignore. Perhaps because you don't return those feelings and you're too kind to outright reject me. But know that when I say I love you, it's because the sun does not rise for me until I see you. The stars don't shine. When I am more than a day without being near you, it's like someone has stolen my joy. And when I do see you, I cannot breathe for it."

The words were so beautiful, like poetry falling from the lips of a fallen angel. And they wrapped around her heart and suddenly she smiled. She couldn't stop smiling as she moved even closer.

"You think I don't return your feelings?" she said, and reached up to touch his cheek. "Sebastian, I think I've been in love with you from the very first moment I saw you all those years ago. I have loved you from afar and valued every stolen moment and conversation, guarding them and reviewing them like a miser with a ledger. Once you turned your regard on me, it felt like I was alive for the first time. That had nothing to do with Claudia's list and everything to do with you. I adore you. I love you."

His entire face lit up with relief and joy, excitement and a glimpse of a future she never could have imagined in her lonely life. He caught her by the waist and drew her to him, his mouth finding hers with passion, but oh, yes, with love. She lifted to him, her hands gripping at his shoulders, trying to find purchase but instead getting swept away.

He pushed her back toward the billiards table and she hit the edge, her legs parting to allow him a place to step between. Her skirts rustled and she sighed against his mouth as he leaned into her with a hungry moan.

They didn't have to speak in that heated moment. Her hands found his fall front, his shoved up her skirt, caressing her stocking-clad thighs as he moved her chemise out of the way.

The first thrust filled her and she ground against him with a shuddering sigh. She had missed this, missed him, missed the physical manifestation of her feelings. Now she recognized it was the same physical manifestation of his. He was gentle as he took, his love plain with how he held her, kissed her, moved through her and against her so that she could find pleasure.

And oh, she did. With every grinding thrust, sensation built between her legs and she gripped them tighter around his hips as the powerful waves of pleasure at last broke within her. She gasped out his name, her body rippling in waves around him. He watched her, drinking in her pleasure as she gave it over without hesitation. And only when she had gone limp beneath him did he thrust harder, seeking his own release as she took his mouth again and sucked his tongue.

"Fuck," he muttered against her lips, and she felt him spend, this time deep within her. And oh, how much better it was to have an encounter end like that, with them fully united in such a way.

He lowered her fully against the tabletop and then somehow managed to wedge himself next to her. She looked at him with a smile when she'd found her breath.

"So that's billiards?"

He tilted his head back and laughed, the sound warming her as much as his arms when he put them around her and tugged her in for another kiss.

"I think we'll have to try teaching you again later," he said.

"No, I'm crossing it off my list. This is billiards as far as I'm concerned," she said.

"Good, then we'll have to play regularly once we're wed," he said, and sat up a little to look down into her face. "If you'll have me. I probably should have asked you this before I got carried away, but that's what you do. Carry me away."

Tears stung her eyes as she looked into the handsome face of this man she had believed would never see her. And now he did. And he was all she saw. The beauty of him and then, even more powerfully, the life they would build together.

"I will," she said. "I *will* marry you, Sebastian, with a very happy heart."

He brought his mouth down to hers again and she lost herself because she knew he would always find her. And she would find him. Until her dying breath.

EPILOGUE

They announced it to Aunt Beulah and Finn first, of course. Marianne had braced herself for her brother's renewed anger, but she'd been surprised that he had accepted the engagement with nothing but what seemed like true happiness. Now she followed him out onto the terrace after their celebratory supper and found him staring up at the stars, a frown on his face.

"How are the stars tonight?" she asked as she stepped up next to him.

Finn shot her a quick smile. "Lovely as always. But nothing compared to you. Love becomes you, Mari."

"I do love him."

"I know. And I think he truly loves you." He glanced back into the parlor where Sebastian was making their aunt laugh with what had to be ribald tales judging from her pink cheeks. "How could I deny you that?"

She took his hand. "Now I hope you can find the same."

Something troubled crossed her brother's expression but then he smiled it away and turned her toward the parlor where they would return. "You worry about your own joy, my dear. That's all you need do to see me happy."

They entered the parlor together and Sebastian stood, his gaze locking on hers immediately. Finn cast her a side glance and muttered, "See, entirely besotted."

He stepped away and went to their aunt, allowing Sebastian to cross to her and take her hand. "I think we should have a very short engagement," he said with a wicked wink at her.

She laughed. "As tempting as that is, I think I'd like to show you off as my fiancé for a while. Let everyone be vastly jealous about the prize I've won."

"You're the prize. But I'm happy to be at your service. Perhaps we can complete Claudia's list. I'm sure we could fill your dance card at the engagement ball we'll hold soon."

She smiled. "As much as I love you for wanting to grant me that, I think I'd rather start our own list. A list for what we want for our life together."

"Oh, very interesting," Sebastian said. "You mean how I'd like to make love to you in every room in every estate I own?"

She shivered at that thought, even as she slapped at his chest. "Certainly, we can put that on the list. But I was thinking more about seeing some of the world together."

"Ah, I see. Well, then I'd like to add dance with you in the moonlight in our garden."

She smiled. "That's a very nice one. What about learning duets on the pianoforte and making guests absolutely sick by how in love we are when we play them together?"

He chuckled. "I'm terrible with any instrument, so I might make them sick with my lack of talent. But I will soldier through bravely if it makes you look at me like you are now."

"I will never stop looking at you like I am now," she said, and then she lifted up on her tiptoes and kissed him, propriety be damned. Because there was nothing else in her world in that moment but him.

EXCERPT OF THE HELLION'S SECRET

ABOUT AN EARL BOOK 2

E sme Crawford sat at the bar in the back of the infamous Donville Masquerade, letting the sights and the sounds of the club wash over her. There were few places in the world where she felt comfortable, but here, with a mask fitted over her face, where she could be anonymous, was one of them. She wore many masks, after all. She was most comfortable where she could be observed but not truly seen.

She almost laughed, for two years ago she would have been anything but comfortable at a notorious sex club, with attendees participating in the most shocking of activities all around her. When she'd first come here, not quite innocent anymore, but certainly not jaded, she had merely stared, shocked that such things could make her feel so tingly all over. But over time, she'd allowed herself to participate. To enjoy more and more. It had made life so much more bearable.

She smiled as one of the barkeeps stepped up. A handsome man with a plain mask and a flirtatious way. "And what can I get for such a lovely lady?"

"Whisky," she said with a wink. "Rivers' best."

He inclined his head and poured it for her. He looked like he might stay and talk, perhaps she could even convince him to leave his post and come in the back for an anonymous encounter that would slake a physical need, but he was signaled by another patron and he sighed as he slipped away.

Esme turned her attention back to the crowd. This would be her only drink tonight, she was too clever to lose control over herself, so she savored it. She took slow sips as she allowed herself to be aroused by the crowd around her.

At one of the gaming tables to her left, a woman was passionately kissing a man as they played cards, her arm moving under the table like she was fondling him. Straight ahead of her on the dancefloor, a gentleman cupped a lady hard against him, massaging her backside as they staggered to the music, oblivious to those around them. She turned her attention to her right where other tables for drinks and conversation...or other activities were spread in a small area near the bar. Many were taken up by couples or more, talking or touching or even fucking in the case of one group.

But in the center of it all was a man, seated alone, wearing a black mask adorned with a few scattered diamonds across the bottom edge. So rich, probably. A gentleman. He was well-favored, with an angled jaw and full lips. And he was watching her, his dark eyes sweeping over her from afar. She smiled and he stood, a slow unfolding of a tall, broad-shouldered body that looked very fine even with all those pesky layers of clothing covering it.

Oh yes, if he wanted to play, it looked like a very good time to be had. He stepped closer and she leaned an elbow on the bar behind her, casual even as she devoured every step he took. When he reached her, he tilted his head.

"Good evening."

She froze, all erotic thoughts and fantasies fading in the moment she heard his voice. She knew it. It came from a different life, one she had fled. One she continued to flee. And if he realized who she was, everything she'd built could come crashing down around her in an instant.

Find The Hellion's Secret (Finn's story) at retailers everywhere soon!

ALSO BY JESS MICHAELS

Theirs

Their Marchioness

Their Duchess

Their Countess

Their Bride

Their Viscountess

The Kent's Row Duchesses

No Dukes Allowed

Not Another Duke

Not the Duke You Marry

Regency Royals

To Protect a Princess

Earl's Choice

Princes are Wild

To Kiss a King

The Queen's Man

The Three Mrs

The Unexpected Wife

The Defiant Wife

The Duke's Wife

The 1797 Club

The Daring Duke

Her Favorite Duke

The Broken Duke

The Silent Duke

The Duke of Nothing

The Undercover Duke

The Duke of Hearts

The Duke Who Lied

The Duke of Desire

The Last Duke

To see a complete listing of Jess Michaels' titles, please visit:

http://www.authorjessmichaels.com/books

ABOUT THE AUTHOR

USA Today Bestselling author Jess Michaels likes geeky stuff, Cherry Vanilla Coke Zero, anything coconut, cheese and her dog, Elton. She is lucky enough to be married to her favorite person in the world and lives in Oregon settled between the ocean and the mountains.

When she's not trying out new flavors of Greek yogurt or rewatching Bob's Burgers over and over and over (she's a Tina), she writes historical romances with smoking hot characters and emotional stories. She has written for numerous publishers and is now fully indie.

Jess loves to hear from fans! So please feel free to contact her at Jess@AuthorJessMichaels.com.

Jess Michaels offers a free book to members of her newsletter, so sign up on her website:
http://www.AuthorJessMichaels.com/

facebook.com/JessMichaelsBks
instagram.com/JessMichaelsBks
bookbub.com/authors/jess-michaels

Printed in Great Britain
by Amazon

48575011R00138